**His kiss had been like nothing she'd ever experienced. It had made her melt. And if it had been anyone but Gavin she would have taken it a little bit further.**

Since their stolen kiss and her panicked reaction to it she'd tried to get her mind off it. Only she couldn't. All she thought about was the feel of his lips against hers, his stubble tickling her chin, his tongue in her mouth, his fingers in her hair.

Her knees knocked and she felt herself swooning like some lovelorn heroine in a romance novel.

She'd been berating herself for walking away, and she couldn't face being alone in her apartment reliving that kiss over and over again. So she went back to work on Monday instead of taking the rest of her time off. Janice didn't even question her early return to work. Virginia often came in on her days off.

Truthfully, Virginia didn't want to admit to her or to anyone else that she just couldn't stand the oppressive loneliness of her apartment and Gavin invading her dreams, her thoughts, her every waking moment.

One kiss had made her realise how lonely she was.

**Dear Reader**

Thank you for picking up a copy of MELTING THE ICE QUEEN'S HEART. I don't think authors can ever truly express how much it means to us that readers like you enjoy our stories.

MELTING THE ICE QUEEN'S HEART is set in one of my most favourite cities of the world: San Francisco. My grandmother had a painting in her dining room of the Golden Gate Bridge and I used to stare at it for hours on end. It's now in my home.

I always wanted to go to San Francisco, and in 2008 at a Romance Writers of America conference I had that chance. It was amazing, and I knew I had to set a romance in that city some day.

This story is about two stubborn surgeons who have never wanted a family of their own because they've both lost someone they cared about deeply and it has made them afraid to love.

Yet somehow love always finds a way, and even the most stubborn man can melt a heart of ice.

I hope you enjoy MELTING THE ICE QUEEN'S HEART. I love hearing from readers, so please drop by my website www.amyruttan.com or give me a shout on Twitter @ruttanamy.

With warmest wishes

*Amy Ruttan*

# MELTING THE ICE QUEEN'S HEART

BY
AMY RUTTAN

Published in Great Britain 2014
by Mills & Boon, an imprint of Harlequin (UK) Limited,
Eton House, 18-24 Paradise Road, Richmond, Surrey, TW9 1SR

© 2014 Amy Ruttan

ISBN: 978 0 263 24176 1

Born and raised on the outskirts of Toronto, Ontario, **Amy Ruttan** fled the big city to settle down with the country boy of her dreams. When she's not furiously typing away at her computer she's mom to three wonderful children, who have given her another job as a taxi driver.

A voracious reader, she was given her first romance novel by her grandmother, who shared her penchant for a hot romance. From that moment Amy was hooked by the magical worlds, handsome heroes and sigh-worthy romances contained in the pages, and she knew what she wanted to be when she grew up.

Life got in the way, but after the birth of her second child she decided to pursue her dream of becoming a romance author.

Amy loves to hear from readers. It makes her day, in fact. You can find out more about Amy at her website: www.amyruttan.com

**Recent title by the same author:**

SAFE IN HIS HANDS

**These books are also available in eBook format from www.millsandboon.co.uk**

This book is dedicated to one of my best friends, Diane. You are so strong and my awe and admiration of you is so much I can't even begin to explain it. Love you.

And to a great friend, Chris. There are friends you make who you feel like you've known your whole life in just a few short moments upon meeting. You were one of them. My family and I miss you every day, Mr. Baxter.

# CHAPTER ONE

"WE HAVE A state-of-the art facility here at Bayview Grace and we're staffed with some of the top surgeons in the country." Dr. Virginia Potter gritted her teeth, but then flashed the board of directors and investors the best smile she could muster.

She hated this aspect of her job, but as Chief of Surgery it was par for the course. She'd rather have her hands dirty, working the trauma floor with the rest of the emergency doctors, but she was used to schmoozing. Earning scholarships and being on countless deans' lists had helped her perfect the fine art of rubbing elbows. It's how she'd got through school. Her childhood certainly hadn't prepared her for that.

Still, Virginia missed her time on the floor, saving lives. She still got surgery time, but it wasn't nearly as much as she used to get.

*This is what you wanted,* she reminded herself. It was career or family. There was no grey area. Her father had proved that to her. He had spent more time with his family instead of rising up in his job and because of that and then an injury he had been the first to be let go when the factory had moved its operations down south. Virginia had learned from that. To be successful, you couldn't have both.

It was the values her father had instilled in her. To always strive for the best, go for the top. Again, that was a sacrifice one had to make. It was a position she wanted.

To not make the same mistakes in life he had. Keep a roof

over your head and food on the table. That was what she had
been taught was a mark of success.

*Others have both.* She shook that thought away. No. She
didn't want a family. She couldn't lose anyone else. She
wouldn't risk feeling that pain again.

"I'd really like to see the hospital's emergency department,"
Mrs. Greenly said, breaking through Virginia's thoughts.

*Anywhere but there,* her inner voice screamed, but instead
Virginia nodded. "Of course. If you'll follow me?"

*Why?* Her stomach felt like it was about to bottom out to
the soles of her feet. Virginia had planned to steer clear of the
emergency room. There were so many more "tame" departments at Bayview Grace.

Departments with Attendings who were more polished and
less dangerous to her senses.

Bayview Grace's ER Attending was the quintessential bad
boy of the hospital.

She led the investors and the board of directors towards the
emergency department and tried to think back to the posted
schedule and whether Dr. Gavin Brice was scheduled for the
day shift, because even though Dr. Brice was a brilliant surgeon he and the board of directors didn't see eye to eye.

*Maybe he's not working?*

Oh, who was she kidding? He was always working and
she admired him for that, except this one time she wished he
wasn't so efficient.

Virginia had been the one to push for them to hire Brice.
They hadn't been impressed with his extensive CV. The board
had wanted a more glamorous, "citified" surgeon. Not one
who'd gotten his hands dirty and lived rough.

*"It's all on your head, Dr. Potter. If Dr. Brice fails, you fail."*
The threat had been clear.

At first Virginia had been nervous, because hiring Dr. Brice
had put her job on the line, but then she'd realized she was
being silly. His work with Border Free Physicians, practicing surgery in developing countries around the world, was an

experience in itself. His survival rates were the highest she'd ever seen.

There was no way Dr. Brice would not succeed at Bay-view Grace.

She'd see to it, but the board still wasn't impressed with him.

His survival rates were still high. Topnotch, in fact, but Gavin was unorthodox and a wild mustang on the surgical floor.

He had no patience for surgical interns. No patience for anyone really.

Gavin followed his own rules when it came to practicing medicine. He was the perpetual thorn in Virginia's side.

*Please, don't be on duty. Please, don't be on duty.*

The board of directors and their investors headed into the emergency department.

"Get out of the way!"

Virginia just had time to grab Mrs. Greenly out of the line of fire as a gurney came rushing by from one of the trauma pods.

*Speak of the devil.*

Gavin Brice was on top of a man, pumping an Ambu bag and shouting orders to a group of flustered interns.

"There's no time, he has a pneumothorax. We have to insert a chest tube." He climbed down and handed the operation of the manual respirator over to a resident.

*Oh. My. God. Did he just say what I thought he said?*

"Dr. Brice," Virginia called out in warning.

Gavin glanced over his shoulder and didn't respond, effectively dismissing her presence. "Get me a 20 French chest tube kit." One of the interns ran off.

"Dr. Brice," Virginia said again. "Think about what you're doing."

The intern returned with the chest tube kit, handing it to Dr. Brice as he finished wiping the patient's side with anti-septic. "Ten blade."

Virginia gritted her teeth, angered she was being ignored. She spun around and gauged the expressions of the board members. Most had nasty pallors. Mrs. Greenly looked like she was about to pass out.

"Dr. Brice!"

"I said ten blade! Have you actually studied medicine?" he barked at an intern, ignoring Virginia.

She stepped towards the gurney. "You can't place that chest tube here, Dr. Brice. Take him to a trauma bay or an OR, stat!"

"Dr. Potter, there are no rooms free and I don't have time to mince words. As you can see, this man has sustained crush injuries and has pneumothorax from a motor vehicle accident. He could die unless I do this right here, right now."

"I really think—"

Gavin didn't even look at her as he cut an incision in the man's chest and inserted the chest tube. "Come on, damn you!"

Virginia watched the patient's vitals on the monitor. It didn't take long before the man's blood pressure and systolic regulated and for the fluid to start to drain through the silicone tube.

"Great. Now we need to clear an OR, *stat*." Gavin shot her a look. One of annoyance. He shook his head in disgust as the trauma team began to wheel the man off towards the operating rooms, his hand still in the patient's chest.

All that was left in his wake was a spattering of blood on the floor from where he'd made the incision to insert the tube.

Virginia rubbed her temples and turned to the board and the investors. "Well, that's our ER. How about we end this tour here and head back to the boardroom?"

It was probably the dumbest thing she'd ever said, but she didn't know how to recover from this situation. In her two years as Chief of Surgery this had never happened to her before. She'd never had an emergency play out in front of the board in the middle of a tour.

Investors had never had to watch a chest tube be inserted in front of them before.

The stunned members nodded and headed out of the department, except for Mr. Edwin Schultz—the tight-lipped head of the board. Another thorn in her side. It was no secret that he thought the hospital was bad from a business perspective. He was the one holding Bayview Grace back, because as far as Virginia was concerned, Edwin Schultz wanted to drop the axe on her hospital.

"Dr. Potter, I'd like to speak with you about Dr. Brice in private."

"Of course," Virginia said, rolling her eyes when his back was turned. She opened a door to a dark exam room, flicked on the lights and ushered Mr. Schultz inside. When she had closed the door, she crossed her arms and braced for a verbal onslaught of tsunami proportions.

"What was that?" Mr. Schultz asked.

"A pneumothorax. The chest tube insertion probably saved the man's life."

"Can you be certain?"

"If Dr. Brice hadn't have performed that procedure, the patient would've certainly died."

Mr. Schultz frowned. "But in the middle of the ER? In front of the investors and other patients?"

"It wasn't planned, if that's what you're implying." Virginia counted to ten in her head. Her whole body clenched as she fought back the urge to knock some common sense into Edwin Schultz's addled brains.

"I didn't say it was, Dr. Potter." He snorted, pulling out a handkerchief to dab at his sweaty bald head. He folded it up again and placed it in his breast pocket. "I'm suggesting that maybe you should have a talk with him about the proper place to perform a medical procedure."

She wanted to tell Schultz that sometimes there was no time to find a proper room or an OR in trauma surgery when a life was at stake, only that wasn't the diplomatic way and she'd worked so hard to become one of the youngest chiefs at Bayview Grace, heck, one of the youngest in San Francisco at the age of thirty. She wasn't about to give that up. Job stability was all that mattered.

Her career was all that mattered.

"I'll have a talk with Dr. Brice when he's out of surgery."

Mr. Schultz nodded. "Please do. Now, let's go take care of the investors because if they don't invest the money we need, the emergency department will have to be cut."

"Cut?" Virginia's world spun around, her body clenching again. "What do you mean, cut?"

"I was going to speak to you later about this, but the hospital is losing money. Many members of the board feel that Bayview Grace could make a lot more money as a private clinic. The emergency department is the biggest detriment to the hospital's budget."

"We're a level-one trauma center." And they had just got that distinction because of two years of her blood, sweat and tears.

Mr. Schultz sighed. "I know, but unless we get the investors we need, we have no choice."

Virginia cursed under her breath. "And how do you feel, Mr. Schultz?"

"I think we should close the emergency department." The head of the board said no more and pushed past her.

Virginia scrubbed her hand over her face.

*What am I doing?*

As a surgeon, she wanted to tell Mr. Schultz what she thought about shutting down Bayview Grace's ER, but she didn't. She held her tongue, like she always did, and her father's words echoed in her ear.

*"Don't tick off the boss man, darling. Job security is financial security."*

And financial security meant food, home and all the necessities.

Virginia wanted to hold onto her job, like anyone did. She wouldn't wish a life of poverty like she'd endured as a child on her worst enemy.

So she was going to hold her head up high and make sure those investors didn't walk away. She was going to make sure Bayview's ER didn't close its doors so the people who worked in trauma didn't lose their jobs.

Though she respected Dr. Brice and his abilities, she knew she had to rein him in to keep control of her hospital.

She just didn't know how she was going to do that, or that she really wanted to.

"Where's the family?" Gavin asked the nearest nurse he could wrangle.

"Whose family?" the nurse asked, without looking up from the computer monitor.

Gavin bit back his frustration. He knew he had to be nicer to the nurses. At least here he had them.

"Mr. Jones, the man with the crush injuries who had the pneumothorax."

The nurse's eyes widened. "In the waiting room. Mrs. Jones and her three teenage sons. They're hard to miss."

"Uh, thank you…"

The nurse rolled her eyes. "Sadie."

"Right. Thanks." Gavin cursed inwardly as he ripped off his scrub cap and jammed it into a nearby receptacle. He should really know her name since he'd been working with her for six weeks, but Gavin couldn't keep anyone's name straight.

*Except Virginia's.*

It wasn't hard to keep her name straight in his head. The moment he'd met her, his breath had been taken away with those dark brown eyes to match the dark hair in a tidy chignon. She was so put together, feminine, like something out of a magazine, and then she spoke about all the rules and regulations, about everything he was doing wrong, and it shattered his illusion.

No wonder the staff called her Ice Queen. She was so cold and aloof. There was no warmth about her. It was all business.

The woman was a brilliant surgeon, he'd noticed the few times they'd worked together, but she was always slapping his wrists for foolish things.

*"It's not sanitary. Legal is going to talk to you. The hospital could get sued,"* Virginia had stated.

In fact, when he had a moment, he planned to discuss the functionality and the layout out of this emergency department with her and the board.

It was horrendous.

When he'd been working in the field, in developing countries, everything he'd needed had been within arm's reach, and if it hadn't been then he'd made do with what he'd had and no one had complained. No one had talked about reprimanding him.

He'd been free to do what he wanted to save lives. It's why he'd become a trauma surgeon, for God's sake.

If he wasn't needed in San Francisco, if he had any other choice, he'd march into Virginia's office and hand in his resignation.

Only Lily and Rose stopped him.

He was working in this job, this suffocating, regimented environment, because of them. He didn't blame them; it wasn't their fault their mother had died. It's just that Gavin wished with all his heart he was anywhere but here.

Although he liked being at home with them. He wanted to do right by them. Give them the love and security he'd never had.

Gavin stopped at the charge desk and set Mr. Jones's chart on the desk to fill out some more information before he approached the family with news.

"You know that was the board of directors you traumatized today," Sadie said from behind the desk.

Gavin grunted in response.

What else was new?

*Board of directors.* He pinched the bridge of his nose. "I suppose Dr. Potter wants to have a little word with me?"

"Bingo." Sadie got up and left.

Gavin cursed under his breath again. "When?" he called after her.

"Ten minutes ago," she called out over her shoulder.

*Damn.*

Well, Virginia would have to wait.

He had to tell Mrs. Jones her husband, who'd sustained severe crush injuries in a car accident, was going to be okay.

All thanks to his minor indiscretion over the chest tube insertion in front of the board.

Only he wouldn't get any thanks. From Mrs. Jones, yes, but from the people who ran this place, no.

It would be another slap on the wrist. Potter would tell him again how he was skating on thin ice with the board of directors.

It would take all his strength not to quit. Only he couldn't.

No other hospital in San Francisco was hiring or had been interested in him. He didn't have a flashy CV after working as a field surgeon for Border Free Physicians.

He didn't make the covers of medical journals or have some great research to tempt another hospital with.

All he had were his two hands and his surgical abilities.

Those two hands had saved a man today, but that wasn't good enough for the board. The bottom line was the only thing that mattered and it made him furious.

If it wasn't for the girls, he'd quit.

He couldn't uproot them. He wouldn't do that to them, he wouldn't have them suffer the same life he and Casey had endured as army brats, moving from pillar to post, never making friends and having absentee parents who had both been in the service.

Although he understood his parents now. He respected them for serving their country and doing their duty. He lived by the same code, only he wasn't going to raise a family living out of a backpack, and because he loved his life and his work he'd never planned on settling down.

He planned to die doing what he loved. Like his father had done.

Working until he'd dropped.

Of course, that had all changed seven months ago when Casey had called him.

Casey wanted stability for her girls and that's exactly what Gavin was going to give them.

Stability.

He picked up Mr. Jones's chart and headed towards the waiting room.

Virginia could wait a few moments more and he'd smooth things over with the board. Mrs. Jones, however, wouldn't wait a second more.

# CHAPTER TWO

*HE'S GOOD PR for the hospital.*

Virginia felt like she was running out of ways to praise Dr. Gavin Brice to the board of directors. None of them were physicians.

None of them understood medicine.

And because none of the board understood medicine she constantly had to explain to them the actions of Dr. Brice; just like she'd done for the past hour.

Virginia rubbed her temples, trying to will away the nagging headache that gnawed her just behind her eyes.

It'd been grueling, but she'd managed to smooth things over. By again reminding them of Dr. Brice's phenomenal survival rate. It was probably that way because of the unorthodox techniques he used.

Of course, what was the point when the head of the board seemed so keen to shut down the hospital's emergency department and make Bayview Grace a private hospital? Private meant only for the wealthy.

And catering only to the wealthy made her sick.

When she'd first decided to become a doctor she hadn't just want to help those who could afford it. It was one of the reasons she'd chosen Bayview to do her intern and residency years. Bayview, back then, had had a fantastic pro bono fund and a free clinic.

The free clinic had been closed two years ago when she'd

done her boards. When she'd become chief she'd tried to get it back, but that would have meant dipping into the pro bono money and that money had been needed.

Mr. Schultz had feigned regret, but Virginia had seen those dollar signs flashing in his eyes. It made her feel a bit sick.

Her stomach knotted as she thought about the countless people from all walks of life who came to her hospital. The pro bono budget was dwindling and she wished she could help more, because at one time in her life she'd been in the poorest of the poor's shoes, getting by on only sub-par medical care.

It was why her sister Shyanne had died.

Shyanne had hidden her pregnancy from her parents, knowing they couldn't afford to help her with medical bills, but the pregnancy had turned out to be ectopic. Virginia had happened to be home on a school break in her first year of medical school and had kicked herself for not seeing the signs early enough.

By the time the ambulance had come to take Shyanne to the hospital, she was gone. Ruptured fallopian tube. She'd bled out too fast.

It was one reason why Virginia donated so much time to the pro bono cases, why she didn't want Bayview's ER closed, like the free clinic had been closed.

There was a knock on her office door, but before she could answer the man in question swaggered into the room and she had to remember herself. She had to control the flush that was threatening to creep up her neck and erupt in crimson blooms in her cheeks.

It was a damn pain in the rump that she was basically his boss and that he was so devilishly sexy. Reddish-gold hair, green eyes like emeralds. Even the scar on his cheek, which just grazed that deep, deep dimple, made the young woman she'd buried under her businesslike façade squeal just a little bit. He was the quintessential bad boy and she'd always had a soft spot for bad boys. Even though her mother had warned her not to give them the time of day.

Virginia and Shyanne had listened. Shyanne had got involved with a good boy. One who had been a golden son of De Smet, South Dakota. A golden son who had knocked Shyanne up and taken off on a football scholarship, leaving Shyanne in the lurch.

"You wanted to see me, Dr. Potter?"

"Yes. Please, take a seat." Pulling at the collar of her blouse, she motioned to the seat in front of her desk. When he moved closer she caught a whiff of his scent. A clean scent of something spicy but rugged and the smell made her insides flutter. With a calming breath she folded her hands neatly in front of her on her blotter. "The board has asked me to speak with you."

A brief smile quirked on his lips as he sat down. "Again?"

"Yes. Are you surprised?"

"Not really.I did happen to catch the expression of some of those investors today."

"You think it's funny?"

Gavin cocked his head to one side. "A bit."

Virginia bit her lip and silently counted to ten. "I managed to smooth things over."

He rolled his eyes. "Look, can I lay something out for you, Dr. Potter?"

She was stunned. "Of course, by all means."

"I don't care what the board approves or disapproves of. I don't care if they think the way I practice medicine is barbaric."

"I don't think they actually said barbaric, Dr. Brice."

He grinned. "Please, call me Gavin."

Virginia swallowed the lump in her throat. It was the first time since they'd met that he'd asked her to use his first name. Not that they'd had much social interaction, besides work-related conversations, and these seemingly frequent discussions about the board and his disregard for following hospital policies.

"Gavin, if you're unhappy, perhaps there's something we can do, or I can do, to make your practice here better?"

"There's nothing you can do. Frankly, I wouldn't be happy anywhere outside Border Free Physicians."

*Intriguing.* "Then can I ask you a personal question?"

"Of course, but I may not answer."

*Touché.* "Why did you leave Border Free Physicians and apply here?"

Gavin's easy smile faded and his mouth pressed into a thin line, his brow furrowing. Virginia couldn't help but wonder if this was something he wasn't going to answer. In his few weeks here she'd ascertained he was a private man. He didn't socialize with many people, ate his lunch alone and did his job efficiently, as far as Virginia was concerned. Maybe not to the board's approval, but as long as the patients lived and there were no lawsuits she was happy.

"I'm needed here," he said finally. Only that's all he said. No explanation about why he'd applied for the job or why he'd told her he wasn't happy here and wouldn't be happy anywhere but with Border Free Physicians.

So why had he left?

"You look confused," Gavin said, the teasing tone returning to his voice.

"Not confused." *Oh, who am I kidding?* "Okay, a bit confused."

"I'm sorry. I didn't really want to put you in this position."

"You haven't put me in a position, Dr. Brice."

"Gavin."

Heat bloomed in her cheeks. "Gavin. I only want to help you, even if this position is not the one you want."

Gavin nodded his head. "I thank you for that."

"For what?"

"For trying to help, but I really don't think I need it."

"I know it's difficult, you came from a job where you worked in rough conditions and had to think on your feet and quickly, but the board of directors has to protect the hospital's best interests."

"Isn't that basically what all trauma surgeons do?"

Virginia smiled. "Yes, but there are certain rules and regulations that have to take place in a hospital setting. They feel what happened today was inappropriate."

He snorted. "Inappropriate to save a man's life?"

"There are rules and the board is protecting the interests of the hospital."

"So you keep reiterating."

"It seems I have to." She crossed her arms. "Do you understand what I'm saying?"

"The bottom line." That look of disdain returned and he shook his head slightly.

Virginia knew and understood what he was feeling, but what choice did they have?

"Unfortunately."

Gavin stood. "I have to protect my patient's best interests, Dr. Potter. I won't change the way I practice medicine."

"I'm trying to help you." Now she was getting irritated. How could she help someone who didn't want her help? Easy. She couldn't. She was losing an uphill battle when it came to Dr. Brice.

He pulled out his pager and glanced at it. Not looking at her, thus silently ending their conversation. "I appreciate that, but I'm needed back in the ER."

Stunned, Virginia stood as he left and then watched through the glass as he jogged down the hall towards the ER.

*What just happened?*

She slowly sank back down into her chair, feeling a bit like a deer caught in headlights, like someone had just pulled a fast one on her.

The board wouldn't be happy with her for not reining him in, but then again she didn't really want to. Dr. Brice was someone who moved to the beat of his own drum. He annoyed the nurses because he couldn't remember their names, didn't have much time for interns and, yes, performed a medical procedure in front of a bunch of rich investors, but the point was he saved lives.

His curriculum vitae was impressive. As far she was concerned.

His image, his work in Africa, doing surgery on refugees, brought in good press for the hospital. People had a soft spot for good Samaritans.

Even if the board thought he was a bit of a rogue surgeon.

Virginia rubbed her temples. Her tension headache was becoming stronger. Couldn't he see how she was trying to make his transition to a metropolitan hospital setting just a bit easier? There was one thing Virginia took away from this meeting today and that was that Dr. Gavin Brice was a bit of a pompous ass.

*Dammit.*

Gavin glanced at his wristwatch and noticed the time. He was late and Lily was going to kill him. Rose wouldn't, though, she was so sweet, but Lily was a force to be reckoned with. This was the third time he'd missed taking her to ballet lessons and he'd pinky-sworn that he'd be the one to take her this time instead of Rosalie, the sitter.

He had no idea what he was doing and he was a terrible father figure, but that was the crux of the matter—he wasn't Lily's and Rose's father. He was their uncle, but as he was their only caregiver since their mother, his sister, had died of cancer, he was no longer cool Uncle Gavin who sent them postcards from new and exciting locations as he traveled to different developing countries with Border Free Physicians.

Now he was Mr. Mom and not very good at it. Lily, who was eight, had reminded him of it every day for the last couple of months.

*"That's not how Mom did it."*

Rose was four, all smiles, but she didn't say a single word.

It's why he was here, in San Francisco, instead of continuing with Border Free Physicians. He hated not being where he wanted to be, but he'd do anything to take care of those girls.

To give them the home life and stability he and his late sister, Casey, had never had.

After all his nieces had been through, there was no way he could drag them from pillar to post, living rough while he worked. He'd had to give up his life as a field trauma physician and get something stable, reliable and in the girls' hometown.

He needed to give them structure and not rip them away from all they knew. Especially not when their world had been shattered after their mother's recent death and their father's when Rose had been only an infant.

He had to be reliable or he could lose the girls to their paternal grandparents. He'd promised Casey he wouldn't let that happen. It had been only three months since Casey had died and though he'd always said he didn't want to be tied down, he wouldn't give the girls up for anything.

Even though he was a hopeless failure.

A cool breeze rolled in off the bay and Gavin shivered. He pulled his coat tighter. Even though it was August, there was a nip in the air and he still wasn't acclimatized to anything that wasn't subtropical.

He stuffed his hands in his pockets and headed for the grey minivan he'd inherited from Casey. His motorbike was sitting alone and forgotten under a tarp in the garage, because you couldn't ferry kids to and from various dance rehearsals, art classes and Girl Scouts' meetings on the back of a motorcycle.

As he made his way across the parking lot he caught sight of Virginia walking toward her dark, sleek-looking sedan. Gavin paused a moment to watch her move. She was so put together and she moved with fluid grace. Even if she seemed tight, like a taut bowstring most days.

Her dark hair was piled up on her head, not a strand of hair loose. There was a natural look to her and she didn't need to wear garish makeup to accentuate those dark, chocolate eyes or those ruby lips. Her clothing was stylish and professional but sexy. Today it was the pencil skirt, paired with a crisp shirt and black high heels that showed off her slim but curvy figure in all the right places.

She climbed into her car, and just as she was sitting down her skirt hiked up a bit, giving him a nice view of her stocking-clad thigh.

Gavin's pulse began to race. If any woman could emulate the princess Snow White it was Dr. Virginia Potter.

He let out a hiss of disgust; he'd been reading Rose far too many fairy tales if he was comparing the chief of surgery to Snow White.

Did that make him a dwarf? Though the way some of those surgeons and nurses moved through the hospital, it was like they were on their way to the mines for the day.

Virginia drove away and Gavin scrubbed his hand over his face. He needed a beer and to veg out in front of the television for a while.

One of the perks of being in the city.

He drove through the streets in a trance, letting the day's surgeries just roll off his back. When he pulled up into his sister's pink-colored marina-style home in the outer Richmond district, a twenty-minute commute from the hospital, he finally let out a sigh of relief mixed with frustration.

*It had to be pink.*

His whole life seemed to be wrapped up in various shades of pink from coral to bubble gum. At least his scrubs weren't pink.

The lights were all on in the living room above the garage, which meant the girls were home from dance rehearsal. Rosalie's car was on the street outside. The garage door opened and he pulled the van inside, next to his tarp-covered Harley.

*I know, baby. I miss you too.*

He sighed with longing, pulling the garage door down and locking it. Rosalie, having seen him pull up, was leaving as he opened the locked gate onto the street that led to the front door.

"Dr. Brice, how was your day?" Rosalie asked, brightly.

"You don't really want to know. How's Lily?"

Rosalie gave him a broad, toothy grin as she heaved her bag over her shoulder. "You don't really want to know."

"That bad?"

"It's been a rough day for her." Rosalie moved past him to the car. "When is your next shift?"

"Tomorrow, but then I'm not on call this weekend. I don't go back until Wednesday afternoon."

"Ah, a four-day weekend. *Que bueno.* I'll see you tomorrow, Dr. Brice. Have a good night." Gavin waited until Rosalie was safely in her car and had driven away before he locked the gate and headed inside.

The stairs from the entranceway to the main level were scattered with various dance paraphernalia and pink things. As he took a step something squished and squeaked under his feet, causing Rose to materialize at the top of the stairs, scowling with her chubby little arms crossed.

Gavin peeled the rubber giraffe from under his foot. "Sorry, I didn't mean to step on Georgiana."

Rose grinned and held out her hand. Gavin placed Georgiana in Rose's hand. "How's Lily?"

Rose rolled her eyes and then skipped off. Gavin groaned inwardly and dragged himself up the last few steps.

He found Lily sitting at the kitchen table, her chin resting on the table with a dejected look on her face. The same face Casey had made when he'd been taking care of her when their dad and mom had left them while they did their duty to their country.

It made his heart hurt just to think about how much he missed his sister.

"Lily."

Lily glanced at him sideways, her blue eyes so like Casey's. "I know. There was an emergency. I get it."

Gavin took a seat opposite to her. She talked so much like a little adult. "There was an emergency, in fact, a car accident. I had to perform surgery."

"Did you save the person's life?"

"I did."

Lily sat up straight. "Then I guess that's worth it."

*At least someone thinks so.*

"Very mature of you, Lily. Look, after tomorrow's shift I have the next four days off. I'm not on call and I can spend it with you and Rose."

Lily chirked up. "Really?"

"Really. We can go down to the piers, watch the sea lions." Rose skipped into the room then and crawled up on his lap.

"Can we get some clams?" Lily asked brightly.

*Clams? I was willing to offer ice cream...*

"You girls like seafood?"

"Yeah, Mom used to take us down to the fish market all the time. We'd get some seafood and she'd make her famous chowder."

Gavin nodded. "Sure. I'll try to make you guys some chowder. How about you two get ready for bed?"

"Sure." Lily got up and took Rose by the hand, leading her towards the front of the house. When Gavin had made sure they were out of earshot he laid his head down on the table. He had never thought he would be a father because he had always been afraid he would be terrible, like his own father was. Oh, his father was a hero all right, but he'd never hugged them, never complimented them and had never been there. It was the same with their mother and it terrified Gavin to his very core. He didn't want to become like them.

Only Casey had had the same fears about becoming a mother and she had been one of the best.

*God, I miss her.*

He just hoped he was doing right by his nieces.

He owed Casey that much.

# CHAPTER THREE

VIRGINIA PICKED UP Mr. Jones's chart and read Gavin's notes quickly. When she glanced up she could see Gavin through the glass partition in Mr. Jones's room. Mr. Jones was still unconscious, so he needed to be in the ICU, but Gavin was speaking to Mrs. Jones.

At least Virginia assumed it was Mrs. Jones, as the woman had been by Mr. Jones's bedside all night. Which was what the night charge nurse had told her when she had started her shift at five that morning.

"Is everything okay, chief?" the charge nurse at the desk asked.

"Yes, Kimber, everything's fine." Virginia smiled and handed the binder back to her. "Just checking on the ER's newest celebrity before I head into surgery."

"Who?"

"Dr. Brice."

Kimber grinned. "Oh, yes, I heard about the excitement in the ER yesterday. I always miss the drama when I'm off."

Virginia cocked an eyebrow. "Is that so? What did you hear?"

"That Dr. Brice inserted a chest tube in front of the investors." Kimber shook her head and chuckled to herself. "I bet they were impressed."

Virginia didn't say anything else as Kimber walked the file back to where it belonged. Before Virginia had been the Chief of Surgery, she'd had friends and comrades she'd been able to talk to about anything. Now, because of her position, she had to be careful of everything she said.

There was no one she could blow off steam with. No one to vent to.

Except the cactus in her apartment.

Even then it wasn't the most animated of conversations.

She missed the days when she could go down to the cafeteria and sit down with fellow attendings and residents and shoot the breeze.

Heck, she could even talk to the nurses back then.

Now they all looked at her for what she was. Their boss.

Their careers were in her hands.

Kimber returned back. "Chief, really, is there anything I can do?"

*Deal with the board for me?* "No, why?"

"You were staring off into space."

"Thinking."

"About?"

Virginia cocked her eyebrow. "What do you think of Dr. Brice?"

"Dishy." Kimber waggled her eyebrows, but then she instantly sobered. "Sorry, chief."

"Professionally, what do you think?"

"Oh, well…" Kimber hesitated.

"Go on," Virginia urged.

"He's pretty brusque with nurses, doesn't remember our names. Refers to most of us as 'hey you'. Rarely says thank-you. But he's good with the patients and he's a great surgeon."

"Thank you, Kimber."

"Is Dr. Brice in trouble, chief?"

Virginia shook her head. "No, I just wanted to see how well he was getting on with the other members of the staff."

"The answer to that is not well." Kimber walked away from the charge desk, just as Dr. Brice left Mr. Jones's room.

He was staring at his pager, headed right for her. Finally he glanced up and saw her there and his eyes widened momentarily. "Dr. Potter, what brings you to the ICU today? I thought you'd be in more investor meetings."

Virginia gritted her teeth. "No. No meetings today, Dr. Brice."

"Gavin." He flashed her a smug smile, which she wanted to wipe off his face. Instead she ignored him.

"I'm headed for the OR, actually."

"Amazing, I didn't think chiefs of surgery were able to operate."

"I'm a surgeon first and foremost. Now, if you don't mind, I'll be off." She turned from him and headed for the OR suites, but Gavin followed her, keeping pace.

"What surgery are you preforming?"

"A routine cholecystectomy."

"I thought you were a trauma surgeon."

"I'm a general surgeon, but I did work in trauma during my fellowship years. Besides, our ER is staffed with several capable surgeons."

Gavin chuckled. "Not me, though."

Virginia cocked an eyebrow, but continued toward the ORs. "What do you mean?"

"We had this talk yesterday, Virginia. I'm not an asset to Bayview Grace."

"Dr. Brice—"

"Gavin," he interrupted.

She took a calming breath. "Gavin, who said you weren't?"

"You did."

"When?"

"Yesterday, after I saved Mr. Jones's life in front of the board, or have you mentally blocked that catastrophe of public relations proportions from your brain?"

Virginia chuckled. "I never said you weren't an asset. You're a fine surgeon, Gavin, you just have to work on your interpersonal skills." The doors to the scrub room slid open and she stepped inside. Gavin followed her.

*Lord. Just let me be.*

All she wanted to do was this surgery. Here she could clear her head and think.

"Interpersonal skills?" A smile quirked his lips. "In what ways?"

"I don't have time to talk the semantics over with you. I have a choly to attend to, that is, unless you want to scrub in?"

*Please, don't scrub in,* one half of her screamed, while the other half of her wanted to see him in action. To work side by side with him.

"I haven't done a routine choly in…well, probably not since my residency, and it wasn't done laparoscopically. The attendings and indeed the hospital where I obtained my residency weren't up to par with Dr. Mühe's ground-breaking procedure."

"I would love to have you assist, Gavin." Virginia stepped on the bar under the sink and began to scrub.

Gavin grinned, his eyes twinkling in the dim light of the scrub room. "Liar."

"Pardon?"

"You don't want me in your OR. I think you've had enough of me."

"That's true. You've been a thorn in my side since I hired you."

He laughed. "I know."

Virginia shook her hands and then grabbed some paper towel. "I would like to see you work, though. I haven't had the chance to observe you, and the nurses tell me you're a brilliant surgeon."

He raised his eyebrows. "I didn't think the nurses cared much for me."

"They don't." She smirked. "You really need to work on remembering their names."

"Not at the top of my priority."

Virginia shook her head and moved towards the sliding door that separated the suite from the scrub room. "Make it a priority, Gavin. You'll find things run a lot smoother if you do. Are you joining me?"

"I think I'll pass, Dr. Potter. I may be needed in Trauma."

"Virginia." She shot him a smug smile and headed into surgery, both relieved and disappointed that he wasn't joining her.

*I should've gone into surgery with her.*

Gavin was beating himself up over not taking the opportunity to sit in on a surgery with Virginia, the ice queen, even if it had been a routine one.

Emergency had been quiet. Eerily so. He'd resorted to charting, though secretly he was trying to learn the nurses' names but couldn't.

He could remember the most complicated procedure, but when it came to mundane, everyday things like dry-cleaning or remembering a name he couldn't.

What was wrong with him?

Something was definitely wrong with him, because he'd turned down the chance to get to know Virginia by operating with her. She'd been so uptight every time they'd spoken, but this time there had been something different about her.

She was more relaxed, more receptive to gentle teasing.

He'd enjoyed his verbal repartee with her, even if it'd only been for a moment. Gavin had seen the twinkle in her eyes before she'd entered the operating room, that glint of humor, and he'd liked it.

And it had scared him.

He had no time to be thinking about women. The girls were his top priority.

"I won't say what you're thinking, because if I say it we'll be bombarded with a bunch of trauma."

Gavin looked up from his chart to see Dr. Rogerson leaning over the desk, grinning at him. Moira Rogerson was another trauma surgeon, but only a fellow as she'd just passed her boards.

"Pardon?" Gavin asked.

"You know, like how actors don't say 'Macbeth' in the theater."

"Oh, I get what you mean."

ER physicians never remarked on a slow day. If they did it was bad juju and they'd have an influx of patients. Gavin returned to his charting, dismissing Moira.

At least he hoped it gave her the hint. The woman had been pursuing him like a lioness hunting a wounded wildebeest since he'd first set foot in the hospital.

"I was wondering if you'd like to grab a bite to eat with me after work?"

The lioness obviously couldn't take a hint. It wasn't that there was anything wrong with her, she was pretty, intelligent and a brilliant surgeon, but he wasn't interested in her.

He didn't like to be pursued and he wasn't interested in starting a relationship with anyone at the moment.

"I can't."

"Why?"

Gavin sighed in frustration. "I just can't."

"I know you're new to this city. What can you possibly have to do?"

Gavin slammed the binder shut and stood up, perhaps a bit abruptly. "Things." He set the chart down and headed towards the cafeteria. Maybe grabbing some lunch would clear his head.

Moira, thankfully, didn't follow.

Sure, he'd been harsh with her and, yeah, he had an itch that needed to be scratched, but since the girls had come into his life he had to be more responsible.

A year ago he would've taken Moira up on her offer and then some. As long as she hadn't wanted anything serious.

She was attractive.

Now that he had his nieces, he just couldn't be that playboy any more. His dating life could be summed up in two words. Cold. Showers.

In the cafeteria he grabbed a ready-made sandwich and a bottle of water. He was planning to take them outside and get some fresh air when he spotted Virginia on the far side of the cafeteria. It surprised him, as he never saw her in here.

She was sitting in the corner of the cafeteria at a table for two, but she sat alone. She was reading some kind of medical journal as she picked at a salad.

The cafeteria was full of other doctors, nurses, interns, but Virginia sat by herself.

*She's the chief of surgery. The boss.*

The ice queen.

No one would want to sit with their boss at lunch. They wouldn't feel comfortable, and he felt sorry for her. She was so young and she didn't have it easy.

*Just like me.*

He crossed the cafeteria and stopped in front of her. "May I join you, Virginia?"

She looked startled and glanced up at him. "Of—of course, Dr. Potter. I mean Gavin."

Gavin took the seat across from her. "How was your choly?"

"Routine." She smiled and his pulse quickened. He liked the way she smiled and especially when it was directed at him, which wasn't often. "How was the ER?"

"I think you can guess."

"I know. I won't say it."

"I'm trying to work on interpersonal skills, but I'm having a hard time putting faces to names."

She cocked an eyebrow. "You don't seem to have that problem with patients."

He nodded. "This is true."

"You're agreeing with me? Amazing." The twinkle of humor appeared again.

"You're mocking me now, aren't you?"

Virginia stabbed a cherry tomato. "So what's the difference between the nurses and the patients?"

"The patients aren't all wearing the same kitten-patterned scrubs."

Virginia chuckled. "Not all the nurses wear kitten scrubs."

"Well pink, then." Gavin snorted. "Always pink."

"What do you mean by that?"

"Nothing." Gavin didn't want to talk about his nieces. His private life was just that. It was his and private.

"What did you do in Africa? How did you remember names there?"

"It was easy. There were only ten of us at the most at any given time."

"It's a number thing, then."

Gavin swallowed the water he had taken a swig of. "There are so many nurses. I think they're multiplying and replicating in the back somewhere."

Virginia laughed. It was a nice one, which made him smile. "Please, don't tell them you think they're cloning themselves. You're a good surgeon, Gavin, and I'd hate to lose you to a pyre they'd light under the spit they'd tie you to."

Gavin winked. "I'm trying."

"Good." She leaned forward and he caught the scent of vanilla, warm and homey like a bakery. He loved that smell. Gavin fought the sudden urge to bury his face in her neck and drink the scent in. "I have a secret."

"Do tell."

"They wear nametags."

Gavin rolled his eyes. "Ha-ha. Very funny."

Virginia just laughed to herself as she ate her salad. "So, do you have any plans for the weekend?"

He cringed inwardly and then picked at the label on his bottle of water. "Nothing in particular. Are you off this weekend?"

"Yes, surprisingly."

"And do you have plans?"

"I do."

Gavin waited. "Not going to tell me?"

"Why should I? You don't divulge aspects of your personal life."

"Touché." He downed the rest of his water and stood. "I'd

better get back to the ER. It was nice chatting with you, Virginia."

"And with you, Gavin. I hope the ER remains quiet for you for the rest of the day."

A distant wail of an ambulance could be heard through an open window of the cafeteria. Several people raised their heads and listened.

Gavin groaned. "You had to jinx it, didn't you?"

And all that minx did was grin.

# CHAPTER FOUR

VIRGINIA WAS TIRED of sitting in her apartment alone. Not even the cactus could get her mind to stop racing.

The two things on her mind were the board's threat to close the ER and Gavin.

After lunch yesterday she had felt the eyes of the other staff members boring into the back of her skull. They had obviously been shocked that the lone wolf, Dr. Brice, had sat with the ice queen of Bayview Grace, and the kicker had been that they'd both seemed to enjoy each other's company.

Well, ice queens could get lonely too.

Virginia couldn't let a slip up like that happen again. She couldn't afford to have rumors flying around about them.

She'd eat in her office from now on.

At least, that's what she'd decided on during her drive down to the pier in the calm serenity of her car.

Virginia had forgotten how crowded and noisy the pier was. It was a Saturday and it was August.

Tourist season.

The height of it.

All she wanted to do was get some fresh produce and maybe some shrimp down at the pier for dinner later, but she'd forgotten how jam-packed Fisherman's Wharf could be. If she had a nickel for every middle-aged guy in an Alcatraz T-shirt wearing sandals with dark socks hiked to their knees who had bumped into her today, she'd have twenty bucks. At least.

Virginia moved through the crowd towards the pier. Her favorite vendor had a stall right near the edge of the market. Nikos knew her by name, knew what she liked and had her order ready every third Saturday of the month.

She liked the conversation and the familiarity, but it also reminded her of how utterly alone she was. How much it sucked that she'd be returning to her apartment in Nob Hill with only the echo of her own voice, her mute cactus and cable television to keep her company.

*You can't have it all, Virginia.*

At least, that's what she kept telling herself. She needed to keep her job so she could keep a roof over her head and send checks to her parents in De Smet. She'd make sure her younger siblings had a better childhood than she and Shyanne had had. Money was what her family needed. Not her presence, even though her mother begged her to visit all the time. A pang of pain hit her. She missed her twin sister and her family with every fiber of her being.

Only she couldn't earn the money her family needed and take time off to visit them.

A shriek across the market shook her out of her dull reverie and she glanced to the source of the sound. A flurry of pink could be seen in the midst of the crush of locals and tourists.

The cloud of pink, in the form of a very puffy and frilly tutu, was attached to a golden-haired cherub on the shoulders of someone one could only assume was her father.

A pang of longing hit her and hit her hard.

Kids weren't part of the plan. It was why she was single, but in that moment Virginia couldn't remember for the life of her why.

*Right, because I don't want to have to worry about anyone else. I don't want to lose any one else.*

Another girl was pulling on the man's arm and he turned around.

Virginia let out a gasp of shock to see a very familiar face peeking out from under the tutu. None other than the lone wolf Dr. Gavin Brice.

She hadn't known he was married and with his vehement stance on where he'd rather be practicing medicine, Virginia would never have pegged him for a family man.

The pained expression on his face also confirmed her assumptions. Why hadn't he mentioned his children before? Or the fact that he was married?

Virginia knew she shouldn't get involved, that she should just turn the other way, but, dammit, Nikos would have her shrimp ready. She wasn't going to change her plans just because it might avoid an awkward conversation.

No. She was going to stay on her present course.

Besides, curiosity was getting the better of her.

*"Curiosity killed the cat!"* Her mother's voice nagged in her ear.

*Shut up, Mom.*

"Lily, I think we have everything we need." Gavin's voice was pleading.

"No way. You're missing the key ingredient. Besides, you said we could go watch the sea lions after this."

"Dr. Brice, what a surprise to find you here," Virginia said, interrupting them.

Gavin's eyes widened as he looked at her. His eldest daughter inched closer to him, her keen blue eyes probing her, picking out her weaknesses.

Virginia recognized the look because she'd done the same many a time when she'd been younger. Only Gavin's daughter was giving the stare dressed in a ballet leotard and tutu. Virginia envied her, because ballet was something she'd always wanted to do as a little girl but her parents couldn't afford it.

"Dr. Potter, what a surprise to see you here."

"I always come to the market when I have a Saturday off." Virginia grinned at the little cherub who was peeking out from the top of Gavin's hair. The cherub had a very messy blonde bun on the top of her head, like whoever did her hair had no idea what they were doing. Virginia could feel her heart turning into a great big pile of goo, which was starting to coat the insides of her chest cavity like warm chocolate. "Are you going to introduce me to your daughters, Dr. Brice?"

The eldest snorted. "He's our uncle, *not* our dad."

Gavin nodded. "Yes, these are my nieces. This is Lily. Lily, this is Chief of Surgery at my hospital, Dr. Potter."

Lily's eyes widened, obviously impressed. She stuck out her hand; the nails were a garish color of red, sloppily painted on. Virginia took her hand and it was a bit sticky. In fact, both girls looked a bit of a mess. Just as Gavin appeared to be, which was so different from his put-together appearance at the hospital.

"Nice to meet you, Dr. Potter."

"Likewise."

"And this little one who's latched herself to my brain, apparently, is Rose." Gavin poked at the chubby cherub, but she wouldn't release her death grip on her uncle.

Virginia smiled. "Nice to meet you, Rose."

Rose didn't utter a word, just continued to stare.

"Sorry, Rose doesn't talk," Gavin explained, and then sighed in exasperation.

"Shy?" Virginia asked.

"No," Lily said, piping up. "She hasn't talked since our mom died."

Gavin wished Virginia hadn't run into them. Mainly because he didn't want any of his work colleagues to know about his private life. On the other hand, he was glad he had run into her and she didn't even bat an eyelash after what Lily had blurted out. Not that he would've even recognized her from the polished businesswoman who graced the halls of Bayview Grace Hospital.

Her dark hair, usually pinned up and back away from her face, hung loose over her shoulders, framing her oval face perfectly.

Instead of a tight pencil skirt, crisp blouse and heels, she wore a bulky cardigan, jeans and ballet flats, but the rest, well, it suited her. He liked the relaxed, affable Virginia.

The cardigan he could do without. It hid too much of her curvy figure, which Gavin liked to admire on occasion, like when she wore those tight pencil skirts and high heels. Just thinking about that made his blood heat.

*Get a hold of yourself, Gavin.*

"I'm so sorry to hear that," Virginia said, and he could tell by the sincerity in her voice she really meant it. It wasn't one of those polite obligatory outpourings of grief. Virginia meant it.

Lily was growing bored with the conversation and was gazing around the teeming market. Rose had released her death grip on Gavin's head and was wiggling to get down off her perch to join her sister.

"Thanks," Gavin said, depositing Rose down on the ground beside Lily. He breathed a sigh of relief and stretched his neck.

"Well, I'd better go. I'm going to pick up some shrimp and head back to my apartment."

"That's what we need, Uncle Gavin. Shrimp," Lily piped up.

"Shrimp? I thought it was clams?" he asked.

Lily rolled her eyes impatiently. "Mom *always* added shrimp to her clam chowder."

Virginia chuckled. "Sounds like quite an undertaking."

Gavin lifted the cooler he was holding with his one arm. "This clam chowder is becoming more and more complicated."

"So it seems." Virginia smiled and warmth spread through his chest. He liked the way she smiled. "Well, I'd better go," she repeated.

"Can I come with you, Dr. Potter? I'll get the shrimp we need, Uncle Gavin."

Gavin watched as Virginia's eyes widened, but only for a moment. She appeared nervous.

"Uh, it's Lily, right?"

"Yep! So, can I come with you?"

"Okay," Virginia said, her voice shaking and her expression one of utter shock. Like a deer in headlights.

"That sounds great!" Lily took Virginia's hand and Gavin took a step back, surprised by his niece's familiarity with a perfect stranger. Gavin handed Lily some money and watched as Virginia guided her to a booth on the outskirts of the market. Virginia, though still looking stunned, handled it well.

They were in view the whole time, so there was nothing for Gavin to be worried about. He shook his head over Lily's behavior. She wasn't that open or friendly with strangers usually. Lily didn't like change. She was a creature of habit, but here she was seemingly at ease with his boss and buying shrimp with her.

A tug on his shirt alerted him to the fact Rose needed his attention. "Yes?"

Rose nodded in the direction Lily had gone with Virginia and shrugged. Gavin chuckled and rumpled her hair. "Got me, kiddo."

Gavin wandered closer to the stall. He watched in awe as the old Greek fishmonger doted on Lily. Virginia was so affable, laughing and totally at ease with his niece. There was a natural connection between Lily and Virginia. It made him a bit nervous. He didn't want or need a relationship. He wasn't looking for a mother for his nieces.

*Aren't you?* a little voice niggled in the back of his mind.

It made his stomach knot.

This was not the life he'd planned, but it was what he'd been dealt.

A bag of shrimp was passed over, Lily handed the old man his money and they turned and headed back. Gavin looked away quickly, not wanting to be caught staring at them. Like he was studying them or something.

"Got the shrimp!" Lily announced triumphantly. Gavin set the cooler down and she placed the plastic bag in beside the clams and the container of scallops.

Virginia knelt down. "That's quite a catch."

"I don't think it'll be clam chowder any more," Gavin said under his breath.

Virginia chuckled again and stood up. The scent of vanilla lingered and as she brushed her hair over her shoulder, he was hit with it again.

He loved the scent of vanilla. It reminded him of something homey. Something he'd always longed for as a child.

"I think you're past the realms of a simple clam chowder and headed toward a seafood chowder or a bisque." Virginia grinned.

"What's the difference?" Lily asked.

"Bisque is puréed and chowder is chunky," Virginia replied.

"Definitely chunky," Lily said.

Gavin just shook his head and shut the cooler. "I guess we're making seafood chowder."

Virginia crossed her arms. "Have you ever made chowder before?"

"Does making it from a can count?"

Virginia cocked a finely arched brow. "No, it doesn't."

"Dang." He grinned and was shocked by the next words that were suddenly spewing from his mouth. "Would you like to come over for dinner?"

Virginia was stunned.

*Did he just ask me to dinner?*

How was she going to respond? Well, she knew what she had to say. She had to say no, she was his boss.

"Please, come, Dr. Potter! Hey, maybe you could walk down to pier thirty-nine with us and watch the sea lions?" Lily was tugging on her hand, her blue eyes wide with excitement.

*How can I say no to that?*

She couldn't, but she should.

"I'm not sure, Lily. How about I just walk down to the pier with you? Then I should go home and get these shrimp into the fridge."

"Want to place them in my cooler?" Gavin asked, popping the lid.

Now she had no excuse to bolt. "Sure. Thanks." Virginia set her bag in the cooler. They made their way through the crowd and onto the boardwalk, heading away from Fisherman's Wharf and toward the loud barking sounds of San Francisco's famous occupants.

Lily and Rose rushed forward and climbed up on the guard rail to watch the sea lions lounge on the docks, surrounded by sailboats lining the pier.

"I've been here six months and I haven't come to see these guys yet. They're pretty loud."

"They are." Virginia winced as the sea lions broke into another course of barking. Lily laughed outright, but Rose didn't make a sound. She just beamed from ear to ear. Rose was such a little angel, or at least appeared to be. "How did your sister die?"

"Cancer," Gavin answered.

"I'm so sorry for your loss." And she was. If anyone understood, it was her, but she didn't share her own pain. She couldn't.

"Thank you." He gazed at her and butterflies erupted in her stomach. He looked so different today. The navy-blue fisherman's sweater accented the color of his hair and brought out the deep emerald of his eyes. His hair was a bit of a mess from Rose's handling, but the tousled look suited him.

It made her swoon just a bit.

*Get a hold on yourself.*

"Well, I'd better head back to my place." She bent down, opened his cooler and pulled out her bag of shrimp, dropping it in her canvas carryall. "Good luck with the chowder."

Virginia turned to leave, but Gavin reached out and grabbed her arm to stop her from leaving. "I'd really like it if you came to dinner tonight."

"Gavin…" She trailed off, trying to articulate one of the many excuses running through her brain.

*I'm your boss.*

*Do you think it's wise?*

*People are already talking.*

Of course, all those excuses were lame. What did she have to lose? Yeah, she was technically Gavin's boss, but it wasn't like he was an intern or even a resident. He was an attending, the head of trauma surgery, so why couldn't they be friends?

*Who cares what other people think?*

"Okay. Sure, I'd love to come to your place for dinner." She pulled out an old business card and a pen. "Write down your address."

Gavin did just that and handed it back to her. "I know Lily and Rose will be excited to have you join us tonight. We haven't had a real house guest since the funeral."

"What time should I be there?"

"Five o'clock. The girls are on a schedule for sleeping and since it takes me ten hours to get them to fall asleep once they're in bed…"

Virginia laughed with him. "Five o'clock it is. I'm looking forward to it."

Gavin nodded. "So am I. I'll see you then." He picked up his cooler and walked to where the girls had moved down the boardwalk for a better view of the sea lions.

Virginia glanced down at the card. Gavin didn't live very far from her apartment. The shrimp linguine she had been planning to make for herself tonight could wait until tomorrow.

Tonight she'd actually have company to talk to instead of four walls and a cactus.

The first thing Virginia noticed about Gavin's house was it was pink. Very pink. She parked her car and set her emergency brake. She'd been passing time for the last couple of hours, waiting for five o'clock to come.

The thing that struck her was that she was very nervous, like she was a teenager again, going on her first date.

She'd even done her hair and her makeup. So different from her usual Saturday attire of yoga pants, no bra and a tank top.

With one last check in the rearview mirror she got out of the car and opened the back door. Before she'd left the market she'd managed to pick up four small sourdough loaves. She was going to hollow them out so they could serve the soup up in them.

She hoped Gavin was a good cook, but she didn't have much faith in that. The thought made her laugh as she headed towards the gated front door. She pushed the buzzer and waited. As she was waiting she noticed a flicker of the drapes in the bay window above her and she spied quiet little Rose peering at her through the lace.

*Poor little soul.*

The door was unlocked and opened and Gavin opened the gate. "Welcome."

Virginia stepped over the threshold as Gavin locked the gate and then the front door again. He was dressed the same as he had been earlier, but at least his hair wasn't as messy. Still, he looked handsome and it made her heart beat just a bit faster.

"Are you afraid I might escape?" she teased, hoping he didn't hear the nervous edge to her voice.

"No, just force of habit. I'm not used to living in a big city."

"You live in a pretty nice neighborhood but, yeah, I can understand your apprehension." She regretted suggesting he might be nervous when he furrowed his brow.

"You live in a very pink house, Gavin," she teased, changing the subject.

"Yes, well, that's my sister's taste. She always loved the color pink." He began to walk up the steps. "You can leave your shoes on—actually, I'd advise it as I'm not the niftiest cleaner. My maid has the weekend off."

Virginia chuckled and followed him up the stairs to the main floor. Rose dashed out from the living room at the front of the house and wrapped herself around Gavin's leg.

"You remember my boss, Rose?"

Rose nodded and then gave Virginia a smile. It wasn't a verbal greeting, but at least it was a start. It was then Virginia noticed that there was no lingering scent of dinner cooking.

"Did you have some problem starting the chowder?"

"Yeah, as in I have no idea what I'm doing."

"I guess it's a good thing I decided to come tonight. Show me to the kitchen."

Gavin grinned and led her to the back of the house where the kitchen was. Lily was in the kitchen with a battered old recipe book in front of her and looked a bit frantic.

"I can't find it," Lily said, a hint of panic in her voice.

"What?" Virginia asked, setting down the bag of bread.

"The recipe my Mom used. I can't find it." Lily was shaking and Virginia wanted to wrap her arms around the little girl and reassure her that everything would be okay. Only she couldn't. She had never been very good at hugging.

"It's okay. Look, why don't we try out my recipe for tonight? What do you think?"

Lily nodded her eyes wide. "Okay."

"Virginia, you don't have to do that. You're our guest."

"It's okay, Gavin. I don't mind." Virginia hung her cardigan on the back of the chair and pushed up the sleeves on her top. "Lily, you want to help me?"

"Of course!" Lily jumped down from the chair where she was sitting and whipped open the fridge, pulling out various items.

"I didn't know you could cook." Gavin watched as Lily plopped the bags of clams, shrimp and the container of scallops on the kitchen table.

"I have hidden depths." Virginia winked. "Do you have any cream, Lily?"

"Yep!" She ran back to the fridge and pulled out a carton.

"Where are your pots?"

Gavin pulled out a stainless-steel saucepan. "Is this good?"

"Not in the least. Do you have a stockpot?"

"A what?"

Virginia rolled her eyes and began to open random cupboards, finally locating a stockpot in a bottom cupboard. She held it up. "This is a stockpot!"

"Impressive." Gavin pulled out a chair and sat down. Rose was there in a flash and climbing in his lap. "Mind if I watch?"

"Why?" Virginia asked skeptically.

"It's how we surgeons learn, by observation, is it not?"

"Perhaps I'll employ the Socratic method on you while I'm dicing the potatoes." Virginia reached down and began to peel one of the potatoes Lily produced.

"I don't think that's fair. I know nothing about cooking."

"He really doesn't," Lily said. "All he can make is grilled cheese. Rosalie does most of the cooking."

Virginia cocked an eyebrow. "Who's Rosalie?"

"My housekeeper slash nanny slash cook." Gavin poked at the bread. "What's in the bag?"

"Ah, that's a surprise that will have to wait until the chowder is ready." Virginia finished peeling the potatoes and began to dice them. Then she went to work on the onions and carrots. When the vegetables were diced she placed them in the stockpot with some salted water and set them to boil.

"Why would I put potatoes on to boil, Gavin?" Virginia asked as Lily grabbed Rose's hand and led her out of the kitchen. They'd obviously lost interest in making dinner.

Gavin shook his head. "I told you, I'm an observer. I don't adhere to the Socratic method."

"And how do you teach your interns?"

"Shut up." There was a twinkle of humor in his eyes.

"Did you just tell me to shut up?" She picked up the knife and pointed it at him. "Very dangerous, my friend." Virginia went to work on the clams, scrubbing them and shucking them. "I'm afraid your strict bedtime rule will be kyboshed tonight. This is going to take some time to cook."

Gavin sighed. "Well, at least it's Saturday and the summer break, so no school. Would you like some wine?"

"I would love some. I actually brought a bottle."

"We'll save yours for dinner." She took a seat at the table as he set a wineglass down in front of her and poured some red into the glass.

He sat back down and poured some into his own. "I'm glad you came tonight. The girls were so excited."

"Thank you for inviting me." Virginia took a sip of wine. It was good, from a local winery in Napa. "So, where is the girls' father?"

Gavin sighed and fingered the stem of his wineglass. "Dead. He was a soldier, he died in Afghanistan just after Rose was born."

Well, that explained why he'd left Border Free Physicians and taken a job in the city as a trauma surgeon. It hadn't been his choice, he was just doing his duty to his sister and his nieces. It was quite admirable of him to give up his career for two little girls.

"How terrible."

Gavin nodded. "I was on a leave from my work in Africa at the time. I spent a couple months helping Casey out. She was a rock, though, and of course my brother-in-law's parents helped too."

"Do they see the girls often?"

"They do. Their grandfather is a marine and they're stationed in Japan, but they come to San Francisco as often as they can to see them. Last time they were here I just worked double shifts at the hospital and allowed them free rein of the house."

She'd sensed a bit of bitterness when he'd mentioned the grandparents and she thought it best to change the subject.

"What about your parents?"

Gavin's lips pressed together in a firm line and Virginia wondered if she crossed some sort of line. "My parents are dead."

"I'm sorry," she said, trying to offer some sort of apology for prying.

"Don't be."

Virginia was stunned by the way he shrugged it off and cleared her throat nervously.

"I'm sorry. I know I sound heartless but they weren't the most loving of parents."

"No, I'm sorry, Gavin. I shouldn't be prying. It's none of my business."

"You're right. It's not."

# CHAPTER FIVE

His gaze was intense and riveting, making her feel very uncomfortable, but not in a bad way. In a way that was dangerous. If she hadn't been his boss and if he hadn't been working under her she could almost swear he was going to kiss her, or strangle her maybe.

If she hadn't been his boss she might even have kissed him back, but she was and she wasn't looking for a relationship.

Not now. Not ever.

*Why not?*

The question surprised her because she'd never entertained the notion before. The fact Gavin made her question the life path she'd chosen for herself was scary.

Virginia had had passing flings, not many, but the moment the man wanted to take it to the next level and become serious she'd break it off, put up her walls and plug the plug.

All her relationships had a DNR lifeline attached to them.

It was so easy, but looking at Gavin now, feeling the blood rush through her like liquid fire, her stomach bottoming out like she was on a roller coaster, she knew once she'd had a taste of him she'd want more.

Much more, and it frightened her to her core.

A hiss from the pot broke the connection and she got up to stir the potatoes and turn down the heat, hoping he didn't notice the blush rising in her cheeks.

"I hope I didn't offend you, Virginia."

"Why would that offend me? I have a tendency to pry to get to the truth." She looked over her shoulder at him. "It's a bad habit of my job unfortunately."

"I bet it's a pain in the rump to have to deal with all that bureaucratic nonsense that goes on behind closed doors at the hospital."

Virginia snorted and checked on the potatoes bubbling in the pot, before draining half the water away. *You don't know the half of it,* she was tempted to say. Only she had to keep those thoughts private. She couldn't be blabbing about hospital politics to another physician. Not when she was the head honcho. Instead she said, "I'm sure you had to deal with red tape with Border Free Physicians."

"To an extent. Of course, I wasn't getting my fingers slapped for inserting a chest tube in the ER in an emergency situation. Life over limb was the motto."

"Touché." Virginia started stirring the soup. The old first-aider motto was how all doctors should practice in a hospital setting. Lawyers, board members and insurance companies thought differently. Though they wouldn't come right out and say it. She changed the subject. The last thing she wanted to do was talk about work. "Too bad you didn't have any crab. This would be great with some fresh bay crab."

Gavin set down his wineglass, headed to the fridge and pulled out a container. "Left over from dinner last night."

"Awesome." Virginia dumped the crab into the pot. "You're quite a seafood connoisseur."

"Yes, lately I am. It's what the girls like and I try to make them happy."

"You're a good uncle."

"I try to be."

Virginia got lost in his riveting gaze again. This had to stop or she was going to forget her rules completely.

"So, are you going to tell me what's in the bag you brought?" he asked, breaking the silence, much to her relief.

"Sourdough bread. It's the secret ingredient to any good seafood chowder, especially in San Francisco."

"I'm not originally from San Francisco. I'm from Billings, Montana."

"That's…"

"Not exciting in the least." Gavin grinned, that dimple she liked so much puckering his cheek. Heat flushed in hers. She cleared her throat and went back to stirring the soup. "Well, I'd better make sure Rose is still conscious and hasn't passed out from hunger."

When he left the kitchen, Virginia let out a breath she hadn't even realized she'd been holding. What was she doing? This wasn't her. If only her mother could see her now, cooking for a man and two young girls. Her mother would be pleased, because her mother felt she worked too much.

*"You never come home."*

Though there was nothing much to go home for and her parents' double wide trailer in rural South Dakota was quite cramped when everyone was home.

If her mother could see her, she'd be pleased. Especially if she knew how much she was actually enjoying the company.

Gavin watched Virginia from across the table. This was not the cool, aloof and businesslike professional he'd been dealing with yesterday. This woman was not the ice queen.

This Virginia was warm and kind. She had an easy rapport with them. At the hospital there was a tangible barrier between Virginia and the other surgeons. A mix of fear and respect. The woman currently sitting in his dining room was not Dr. Virginia Potter, Chief of Surgery.

Only she was.

He was amazed at how well she got on with his nieces. Lily had been so closed off and cold with strangers since Casey had got sick and died. Even with him it had taken some time for Lily to warm up and trust him.

And you couldn't blame Lily for that reaction. Death had hit her hard, twice, in her young life.

With Virginia, Lily was chatting happily and engaging her in conversation. A smile touched his lips as he watched the two of them talk. Virginia was asking Lily about dancing and school. Was this what it was like to have a real family dinner?

He wouldn't know.

His parents had never been around. Casey and he had lived off of cereal and peanut-butter and jelly sandwiches. Sometimes, when Mom hadn't gone shopping, there would only be enough bread or cereal for one. Those were the nights he'd gone to bed hungry, because he had been taking care of Casey.

Now he was taking care of Casey's girls, making sure they wanted for nothing and that they were happy. It was why he was in the city instead of some far-flung country.

"I think your sister is out for the night. What do you think, Gavin?"

"What?" Gavin asked, shaking those painful childhood memories from his head. "What's up?"

"Uncle Gavin, Rose is passed out in her chair." Lily gazed at her little sister lovingly.

Lily and Virginia were right. Rose was sound asleep, curled up on her chair with her arms tucked under her chubby cheek and her bottom up in the air.

"Lots of excitement today." Gavin pushed out of his chair and scooped his younger niece into his arms. She let out a small huff of air but didn't wake up. "I'll be back momentarily."

"At least she ate her soup, but she didn't get a chance to finish off her bowl," he heard Lily say with an excited giggle as he walked down the hall toward Lily's and Rose's shared bedroom. He smiled again as he remembered the look of pure excitement on the girls' faces when their chowder had been served up in their own individual bread bowls.

*"Bowls we can eat? No dishes!"* Lily had chirped excitedly.

Rose hadn't said a word, but the twinkle in her eyes and the smile on her face had spoken volumes. She had been excited too. He'd salvage what he could of the bread bowl so she could have some tomorrow. Rose would be so disappointed in the morning to find out she'd missed out on her dinner bowl.

Gavin tucked her into the bottom bunk. Lily would climb in beside her sister later. The bunk beds were fashioned for a single on top and a double underneath. Though Lily's bed was technically the top bunk, that's not how they slept.

If they weren't waking up in the night, as far as Gavin was concerned, that sleeping arrangement was fine with him.

He tiptoed out of the girls' bedroom, stepping on the darned rubber giraffe again, but Georgiana's pitiful squeak didn't even cause Rose to stir. Gavin just cursed silently under his breath and made his way back to the kitchen.

When he got there, he could see that Lily wasn't far behind her sister. Her eyelids were beginning to droop and she was leaning pretty heavily on her elbow.

"Hey, kiddo, why don't you get ready for bed?" Gavin suggested.

"Aw, do I have to?"

"I think you should. You were an awesome help to me today, Lily. Thank you," Virginia said, standing and starting to clear the table.

"Okay." Lily got up and dragged herself down the hall to the bathroom.

"Brush your teeth!" Gavin called, and Lily's response was a groan of derision.

Gavin picked up the remainder of Lily's and Rose's dinners and took them into the kitchen. Virginia was filling the sink with water.

"You don't have to do that," he said. "You were our dinner guest and I made you cook."

"I don't mind."

"No, seriously. Come and have another glass of wine while I put the leftovers away."

"One more glass. I do have to drive home."

Gavin chuckled and poured her another glass. "The girls really enjoyed the dinner tonight."

Virginia smiled and warmth spread through his chest. She had a beautiful smile, with her full red lips. If it was any other woman, he'd be putting the moves on her.

*She's my boss.*

"I enjoyed tonight too." She took a sip. "I think there's one thing you need to learn about managing a house full of girls."

"Are you critiquing my parenting skills?" he teased.

"Just a bit."

"What can I approve on, then?"

"Don't take this the wrong way, but you seriously have no idea when it comes to a little girl's hair."

Gavin laughed and she joined in. It was the first time he'd really heard her laugh, a deep, throaty, jovial laugh, which not only surprised him but delighted him too.

"And you do?"

"Yes," she stated confidently. "First, because I was a little girl at one point in my life and also I have two younger sisters."

It was the first time she'd opened up to him. It was the first nugget of information he'd got from her.

"Sisters, eh?"

"Yes." She smiled. "And even though you may have grown up with a sister, you really don't know anything about hair."

"Little girls' hair baffles me. Actually, it drives me squirrely," he said, and he meant it. No matter how many scrunchies or ties or pins he used, he couldn't put their hair up in a bun or braid to save his life, but it was a necessity for dance class. "Anything else?"

"Also the nails. That red color is not flattering on Lily and it's pretty messy."

"Yes, I admit I need some boning up on those finer aspects, but she wanted to paint her nails and I get home from the hospital tired and some nights I don't have any fight in me. I just give in."

Virginia nodded. "I understand about giving in."

Tension settled between them. He wanted to ask her what was stressing her out, but he knew it had something to do with him and what the board deemed his crazy, unorthodox methods. The last thing Gavin wanted to do was talk about work with *this* Virginia.

The laid-back, affable, warm and caring Virginia who had just spent part of the day and the evening with him and the girls.

The Virginia who made him forget about his worries. How he feared he was a terrible father figure to his nieces. That he'd lose them to their paternal grandparents. The girls were all he had left. Only he felt like he was failing them.

Not once since his sister had died had he and the girls enjoyed an evening like this together. It had been nice and he found himself wanting it all the time, even though a long time ago he'd sworn he'd never have a family or a wife, because of the lifestyle he wanted. Living rough and always traveling.

"I should go," Virginia said, breaking the silence that had settled between them. She got up and picked up her purse from the kitchen counter. "Are you sure you don't need a hand with those dishes?"

"Positive. I'll walk you out."

Gavin escorted her to the front of the house and down the stairs. He unlocked the outside gate and stood with her for a few moments. The night was clear and the moon full. The water on the bay was still, like a mirror.

You could see the lights from across the bay, twinkling in the darkness; the two bridges dominating the San Francisco skyline.

"What a beautiful night." Virginia let out a little sigh, which sounded like one of regret. "I should go. Thank you for a lovely evening."

"Thank you for coming." He wanted to say that he'd really enjoyed getting to know her somewhat better, but instead said, "The girls really enjoyed it."

"I enjoyed meeting them." Virginia hesitated and then

ducked her head. "Well, I'd better be going. I'll see you on Wednesday afternoon, Dr. Brice."

And just like that it was no longer Gavin and Virginia.

It was Dr. Brice and Dr. Potter and he didn't like that connection at all.

She turned and walked away from him, heading towards her car. "Wait!" he called out, surprising even himself.

Virginia paused and turned. "Yes, Dr. Brice?"

"What are you doing tomorrow?"

# CHAPTER SIX

*WHAT AM I doing? What am I doing?*

Virginia was standing in the middle of Union Square in the evening, waiting for Gavin and the girls. She'd been so flabbergasted that he'd invited her out, but it wasn't like a date. It was just another outing with Gavin and his nieces. Just an innocent outing between friends.

At least, that's what she kept telling herself.

The plan was to walk up from Union Square to Chinatown and have some dim sum. She had nothing better to do and it was a nice August evening.

Virginia nervously glanced at her watch. They were late, only five minutes but she'd been waiting for twenty, because when she was nervous she was always early, or, as she liked to call it, overly punctual.

*Relax. They'll be here.*

What if they didn't show? She'd appear like a real dork. Virginia shook that thought away. No one knew where she was. No one at the hospital knew she was meeting Gavin and his nieces here.

She needed to get a grip.

"Sorry I'm late."

She turned and saw Gavin, without the girls, behind her. He was dressed in jeans, a sport jacket and a nice button-down shirt. His hair wasn't a complete mess but still stuck up here and there from a troublesome cowlick.

He had a nice five-o'clock shadow, but she liked scruffiness on a man. She could smell the spicy scent of his soap, which made her feel a bit weak in the knees. Gavin presented a neat and tidy appearance but there was a hidden depth of ruggedness to him that appealed to her.

She'd always had a penchant for bad boys, wild boys, but she tended to date respectable, clean-cut men.

For some reason, when she saw Gavin, she pictured him on a big motorcycle clothed in leather and denim as he rode down the California coast. That brief little thought caused a zing of anticipation to race through her, but it was just a fantasy. She knew Gavin drove his late sister's minivan.

"Where are the girls?" she asked, her voice cracking. She winced, worried that she was probably sounding as dumb as she felt at the moment.

"Ah." He rubbed the back of his neck. "Their grandparents flew in unexpectedly from Japan. They have a layover for a couple of days, so the girls are spending time with them."

Virginia just nodded, suddenly feeling really nervous, like a shy teenage girl standing at the edge of a dance floor, waiting for someone, anyone to ask her to dance.

*Why isn't he saying something?*

"Maybe we should schedule this for another night, when the girls are able to join us?"

"Why?" he asked.

Virginia's cheeks flushed. "Do you think it's appropriate for the chief of surgery to go out with an attending?"

"We're going to have dinner, as friends. Just think of it that way, if you're nervous. I think a boss can have a friendly dinner with an employee." He grinned. "We'll save Chinatown and the dim sum for the girls. How about we catch the streetcar and head down to a diner on the Embarcadero?"

Virginia hesitated. "I don't know."

"Come on, Virginia, help me out. I want to give the girls space with their grandparents. Don't make me be a fifth wheel to their time together and I rarely have a moment free without them."

*Go on. Live a little.*

"What the heck. You're right. Lead the way."

Gavin took her hand, her heart beating just a bit faster at the intimacy. His hand was warm and strong as it squeezed hers gently. "Come on, then." He pulled her through the square as they jogged down to catch the F Market streetcar and she was glad she'd decided to wear flats instead of wedges or boots. Flats helped her keep up with Gavin's long strides.

When they crammed onto the streetcar, Virginia finally caught her breath. "Where are we going?"

"Fog City Diner."

"I hope you made reservations. That place is a San Francisco institution."

Then he grinned deviously, like a Cheshire cat. "We'll just have to play it by ear, won't we?"

She was going to say more, but more people got onto the streetcar and they were separated in the crowd.

When their stop came she got off and met him at the back exit. "It was a bit of crush in there, wasn't it? Seeing how you're not from around here, I thought you might miss your stop."

"I'm a pro at public transportation and large crowds. I rode a train across India and stood for six hours. Not fun."

"No, I bet."

They walked toward the diner and from the look of the crush of people going in and out of the doors Virginia knew it would be busy, and there weren't many other options around. The other couple of restaurants nearby would be overflowing with rejects from Fog City.

"Why don't we catch the next streetcar and head down to the wharf?" Virginia suggested.

"You have so little faith." He took her hand again, making her pulse race and her palms sweat.

*Great. Sweaty palms are so alluring.*

"It looks busy," she said nervously.

"Appearances can be deceiving." He pulled her inside and walked up to the seating hostess. "Reservations for two, Gavin Brice."

The hostess checked her list, smiled and grabbed two menus. "Ah, right this way."

Gavin grinned at Virginia with smug satisfaction. "After you."

Virginia shot him a dirty look as she followed the hostess to their booth overlooking the Embarcadero. He slid in across from her, the polished black tabletop reflecting his smug pleasure.

"You had reservations."

"I did. As you said, Fog City is a San Francisco institution."

"It's almost as if you planned this."

"Well, when the girls' grandparents flew in early this morning I made the reservation. I would've told you but I don't have your home number."

"You have my pager," Virginia teased. "Everyone in the hospital has my pager."

"You carry your pager around when you're off duty?"

She pulled it out of her purse and flashed it at him, like the big nerd she was. "I'm Chief of Surgery. What if there was some kind of freak accident and the press swarmed the hospital?"

"High-profile cases don't go to Bayview Grace."

Virginia bit back the feeling of annoyance that was threatening to rise. It was always a bit of a sore spot for her. She'd raised Bayview Grace to a level-one trauma center, but other hospitals still got all the press.

"That's part of my five-year plan for the regeneration of Bayview Grace Hospital. I plan to make it the top hospital in San Francisco. It's well under way."

Gavin leaned back against the cushioned seat. "Does it matter? We're a level-one trauma center and we practice good medicine. Who cares if we're not the top?"

"I care," Virginia snapped. When she'd become Chief of

Surgery at Bayview Grace the hospital had been in a sorry state and it had ranked low on the list of hospitals nationwide and statewide. It had been her mission to change that, to bring back its glory days.

It was what she'd lived and breathed for the first two years in her position. She would fight to the bitter end to keep Bayview open.

Two lonely, busy years and now Gavin was suggesting it didn't matter?

That her life didn't matter?

Gavin regretted the words when he saw the change of expression on Virginia's face. When they'd first got to the diner she'd been smiling so brightly and had been so at ease, just like she'd been the night before.

As soon as he'd brought up the hospital, that amiable woman had been replaced by the workaholic, tight-lipped and controlling chief of surgery that most staff at Bayview Grace avoided.

Virginia was not the most popular surgeon in the hospital, but it was hard to be popular when you were responsible for budget cuts, staffing and all the other mundane administrative stuff that Gavin wouldn't wish upon his own worst enemy.

Tonight wasn't supposed to be about work.

*Then what's it supposed to be about? You're out with your boss.*

It was supposed to be about fun. A night away from the girls and the responsibility of fatherhood.

"Are you saying the hospital's standing isn't important?" she asked, her voice rising an octave.

"That's exactly what I'm saying." No, he didn't care about the hospital's standing. He'd spent years in dirty holes of medical facilities, trying to bring medicine to those people who had no access. He'd worked in sweltering temperatures, monsoons, festering cesspools to treat people.

That's all that mattered when it came to medicine, as far as he was concerned. A hospital rating meant nothing, as long as people were being cured.

"I think I should go." She slid to the edge of the seat, but he reached out and grabbed her.

"Don't go. Look, I know it's important to you, but it's not important to me. I come from a different world."

She eyed him with misgiving but slid back to where she had been sitting.

"I don't want to talk hospital politics."

"Isn't that what coworkers do?" she asked.

"How about, just for tonight, we don't. Let's just forget about it all and enjoy ourselves."

Her expression softened. "You're right. I'm sorry too, for what it's worth."

"Why are you apologizing? You have nothing to apologize for."

"I do. You see, I don't go out. I live and breathe that hospital. I've forgotten what it's like to talk to another adult human being."

Gavin chuckled. "I understand. How about we take it slowly? Hi, my name is Gavin Brice and I'm a fishmonger."

Virginia laughed. "You're a what?"

"You know, one of those guys down at the wharves that monger fish."

"Do you know what monger means?" she asked, cocking a thinly arched brow.

"Doesn't it mean clubbing the fish to death or something?" He made a gesture of beating a fish against the table. "Like bashing in their brains?"

She laughed again. "That's not what a fishmonger does and that's not how you use that word properly in a sentence. It means to peddle, to sell or stir up something that's highly discreditable."

"Well, thank you, Merriam-Webster." He winked.

"What would you like to order?" the waitress asked, interrupting their conversation. Gavin quickly glanced at the menu and ordered the catch of the day and Virginia did the same.

When the waitress was out of earshot he continued.

"So, as I said. I'm a fishmonger. I like screwball comedies and aspire to own a macadamia farm in Hawaii one day and populate it with llamas."

"That's the most absurd thing I've ever heard anyone say."

Gavin grinned. "Come on, play along. Tell me who you are."

"Dr. Virginia Potter."

"No."

"No?" she asked in shock.

"No, you're…" He paused, trying to think of some crazy name.

"Fifi La BonBon?" she offered.

"I like it. It's very French and naughty."

A pink blush colored her cheeks and she cleared her throat. He didn't mean to get so personal with her, but he couldn't help himself. Virginia intrigued him and he wanted to get below the surface of her prim and proper exterior.

Beneath that cool professionalism he knew someone warm existed, a passionate woman, he hoped. By the way her cheeks flushed he was positive one did and his blood fired as he thought about exploring that woman.

Gavin fought the urge to run his fingers through her silky brown hair, to crush those rose-colored lips under his, bruising them in passion as he peeled those crisp, pastel-colored clothes from her body. He cleared his throat and fidgeted in his seat.

*She's your boss.*

It'd been some time for him; yes, that was a fitting explanation for his sudden infatuation with Virginia. A woman who had been a thorn in his side since he'd arrived at Bayview Grace. Always calling him into her office to tell him what he was doing wrong.

*It's not her choice. It's the board.*

But he knew the reason. She didn't chase him like other women did.

"Okay," Virginia said, breaking the silence between them. "I'm Fifi La BonBon and I'm a tank cleaner at the Monterey Bay Aquarium. I spend my day avoiding sharks and tickling starfish."

Now it was his turned to look stunned. "Really? A fish-monger and a tank cleaner, what an interesting pair we make."

The waitress brought them their drinks and caught the tail end of his sentence, shooting them both a quizzical look be-fore disappearing again.

"The waitress is going to think we're nuts." Virginia swirled the wine in her glass. "I've never lived on the edge like this."

"What, wine in a diner?" Gavin teased, taking a sip of his Scotch. "You rebel, you."

Virginia leaned forward across the table and he caught a whiff of her perfume, vanilla. So different from when they were at the hospital, where scents were banned due to allergy reasons. Everything was so antiseptic and sterile.

So not like his work with Border Free Physicians, where every scent known to man seemed to trudge in and out of his clinics. Some intriguing, some not so much.

"No, this fantasy talk. I guess I'm not used to lying."

"Oh, come on, Virginia. You must have to bend the truth to some of your employees sometimes. Don't we bend the truth to our patients one time or another to make the blow sting just a little bit less?"

Her smile disappeared, but only for a brief moment, and he was worried he'd crossed some invisible line again. "Whatever do you mean? I clean tanks."

Gavin laughed out loud, surprised by the way she broke the tension and eased into the icebreaker conversation he'd started. It surprised him and pleased him. The waitress brought their meals and they chatted about their fake personalities, com-ing up with the weirdest stuff they could imagine, until it was time to leave the diner.

There was a chilly breeze coming off the bay when they headed outside and walked along the Embarcadero towards the next pier, where they could pick up the streetcar and head back to Union Square. It was where he'd parked his motorcycle.

"Did you drive down to Union Square?" he asked, because he didn't know exactly where she lived.

"No. I walked. I only live in Nob Hill, not far from Union Square."

*Damn.* He was disappointed. He'd wanted to offer her a ride on his bike, take her to her door, like a proper gentleman would.

*This is not a date,* he reminded himself for the umpteenth time, but who was he kidding? It was. He knew it and he was pretty sure she knew it too. Only it didn't have to be anything more than just this.

They wandered along the Embarcadero in silence. The only sounds were traffic, the waves and the wind, and they finally stopped when they could see the Coit Tower clearly.

"We've wandered quite a piece away from Market Street," she said, and she turned to look out over the water. The sun was setting, just behind the Golden Gate Bridge, in a fiery ball of liquid gold.

"It's been a while since I was able to enjoy a sunset." She let out a sigh. "I've been so busy, so damn busy."

Gavin wondered if he was supposed to hear that last admission, but if he wasn't supposed to be privy to that thought, he was glad he was.

He liked this Virginia. Very much.

"It's a nice sunset," he said. "But it's not my favorite."

"Where was your favorite sunset, then?"

Gavin leaned against the railing of the boardwalk. "Egypt. The sun setting behind the pyramids as the full moon rose above them. It was…magical."

Virginia sighed. "You've been so many places. I envy you."

"You haven't traveled much, I take it?"

She shook her head. "I went to Harvard and then came here. Like I said, I was too busy trying to fix Bayview Grace."

"What about summers off from school?" he asked.

"I worked. Scholarships and what I could save myself paid

my way through. My parents couldn't afford to send me." A blush crept up her neck, as if she was embarrassed by that admission.

"That's a shame."

"You're going to bring up this again?" she asked, annoyance in her tone.

"No, it's just that you haven't traveled or cut loose. I can't imagine not. It's hard for me to stay put and take care of my sister's kids. My wandering foot is itchy."

"You're doing the right thing, giving them the stability they deserve."

Gavin nodded, even if it was a bitter pill to swallow. He knew all about wanting that stability and craving it in his childhood, but it was hard to do when you spent most of your adult life living out of a rucksack. The whole world was your home.

"I can't tear them away from their home. I won't."

Virginia nodded. "I do envy your travels, though."

"You should try it, at least once or twice."

She smiled and ducked her head, tucking a strand of hair behind her ear. "Perhaps one day."

There was a sparkle in her eyes. Maybe it was the way the fading light from the sun reflected on the water but Virginia seemed to glow and Gavin couldn't help himself. He wrapped his arms around her, tipped her chin and kissed her.

He cupped her face in his hands; her skin felt like silk. Virginia softened a bit. The taste of the wine she'd drunk still tainted her lips. It was sweet, like her. He wanted to press her body against his, feel her naked under him. When he tried to deepen the kiss, Virginia pushed him away.

Her cheeks were flushed and she wouldn't look him in the eye. "I think…I think I'd better go."

"Virginia, I'm sorry."

"No, it's okay. There's no need to apologize and there's no need to mention it again." She hailed a cab and it pulled over. She turned, but still wouldn't look him in the eye, obviously mortified by what had happened between them. "I'll see you Wednesday, Dr. Brice. Thank you for the lovely evening."

And with that she climbed into the cab and was gone.

# CHAPTER SEVEN

VIRGINIA LOOKED DOWN and realized she'd been holding the same file for a while. Janice would be furious, because all the "sign here" stickies were still void of her signature. Since Sunday when Gavin had kissed her she'd been walking around in a bit of a haze.

More like a stupor. His kiss had been like nothing she'd ever experienced. It had made her melt and if it had been anyone but Gavin she would've taken it a little bit further.

Since their stolen kiss and her panicked reaction to it, she'd tried to get her mind off it. Only she couldn't. All she thought about was the feel of his lips against hers, his stubble tickling her chin, his tongue in her mouth, his fingers in her hair.

Her knees knocked and she felt herself swooning like some lovelorn heroine in a romance novel.

She'd been berating herself for walking away, and she couldn't face being alone in her apartment, reliving that kiss over and over again. So she went back to work on Monday instead of taking the rest of her time off. Janice didn't even question her early return to work. Virginia often came in on her days off.

Truthfully, Virginia didn't want to admit to her or anyone else that she just couldn't stand the oppressive loneliness of her apartment and Gavin invading her dreams, her thoughts, her every waking moment.

One kiss had made her realize how lonely she was.

Dinner had been so wonderful, as had the company. The walk along the waterfront had been the same. She'd gone on other casual dates with men, but nothing compared to the time with Gavin. Usually she couldn't stop thinking about work.

For one stolen moment she'd forgotten she was Chief of Surgery. She'd forgotten about all her duties, all the problems, everything that made up the core of her existence.

Gavin made her forget everything, made her think of traveling, something she'd always dreamed of, though she'd never entertained the idea of doing it for real. Travel was expensive and a luxury. That was just it, Gavin made her feel frivolous, like doing something more than being a surgeon and working her fingers to the bone.

She couldn't remember the last time she'd enjoyed herself so much.

*I shouldn't have left him. I should've taken a chance.*

Only she knew why she had walked away. It'd been a one-off. When she'd got home and thought about it, she'd realized she shouldn't have done it.

She shouldn't have let him kiss her.

She was Gavin's boss. Nothing could happen between them. They couldn't date.

It was better to put an end to it now, before the girls became attached to her or something, and there was no way she could hurt those girls.

They'd already been put through the wringer enough.

Only a part deep down inside her wanted to risk it all to get to know them better. Gavin was handsome, but it wasn't his looks that attracted her to him and it definitely wasn't that pompous air he had when he marched through the halls of Bayview Grace. Far from it. That Gavin was a jackass.

It was the Gavin she'd briefly got a glimpse of on Saturday at his house. The Gavin who'd kissed her down by the water.

The man who had been thrust into fatherhood appealed to her greatly and that thought scared her. Kids weren't in the plan, she reminded herself for the umpteenth time.

*Why can't they be?*

She was a doctor, she wasn't going to end up poor, like her parents. Even though she could give a child what they needed, she didn't want to risk it.

What if something changed and she couldn't support a child any more? What if something happened to that child? She'd witnessed the pain and suffering her mother had gone through when Shyanne had died. It had almost killed their mother and she never wanted to experience that kind of loss.

It was far too risky.

Her pager went off in her pocket and she pulled it out. She was wanted in the trauma department. For one moment her courage faltered, because it was Wednesday and Gavin would be back on duty and, like the shy wallflower she'd been in high school, she cringed inwardly over the thought of facing him.

*Get a grip.*

Virginia pocketed her pager. She was Chief of Surgery. This was her hospital and she was first and foremost a surgeon.

Just because she was chief and did a lot of paperwork, it didn't mean she didn't belong in the trauma bay, getting her hands dirty.

And she had nothing to be ashamed about.

Nothing to be embarrassed about, because nothing had happened between her and Dr. Brice and that's the way it had to remain.

She had to forget about the kiss. It'd been a mistake and thankfully no one knew about it.

When she entered the trauma bay her gaze naturally gravitated towards Gavin, but she took a step back when she realized he wasn't in his scrubs but in his street clothes. Of course, it was only ten in the morning. He wasn't due to start until two. He also wasn't leading the paramedics, he was traveling with them and on the gurney was a little figure.

Virginia's heart skipped a beat and she ran towards them.

"What happened?" she asked as she followed the gurney into the trauma pod.

"Female age eight, fell off the monkey bars at the play-ground. No obvious head trauma, but there appears to be a fracture of her right ulna," the paramedic stated.

Lily was on the gurney, her face grey with pain. Virginia looked at Gavin and his pained expression said it all. Suddenly she saw her twin sister Shyanne on the gurney in agony, bleeding out. Lily had a fracture. She was not hemorrhaging because of a ruptured fallopian tube.

*Get a grip, Virginia.*

"Glad you could come, Dr. Potter," Gavin said.

"Of course. I'm the trauma surgeon on duty."

Gavin nodded, but didn't look at her.

Lily's gaze met hers. "Dr. Potter?"

"Hi, Lily."

"Wow, the chief of surgery." Then she sat up and retched into a basin.

*I feel the same way some days.*

"Let me just do an examination of your arm." She turned to the nurse and fired off instructions for an X-ray and pain medication.

Lily winced as Virginia gently palpated the site.

"It hurts." A sob caught in Lily's throat, but she kept up her stiff upper lip.

"Yeah, I'm sure it does." She leaned down and whispered, "You can cry if you want. Breaking a bone is a huge deal."

Lily shook her head and glanced at her uncle. "I told him I'd be brave."

Virginia glanced over her shoulder at Gavin and then back at Lily. "We're going to do an X-ray and check out what kind of fracture it is, and Nurse Jo here is going to give you some pain medicine in a moment."

Lily nodded and Virginia walked over to Gavin. "Is she allergic to anything?"

"No. Nothing."

"Good. Where's Rose?"

"With her grandparents. They were supposed to fly out, but

then Rosalie called as I was getting ready for work." Gavin scrubbed a hand over his face. "I appreciate you coming down, but couldn't one of your ortho attendings handle this?"

"No, Lily knows me. I'll make this as painless as I can for her."

Gavin's eyes narrowed. "You don't have to."

"I want to. She's frightened, though she doesn't want you to know it."

Gavin sighed and mumbled thanks before pushing past and sitting next to Lily. A pang of longing hit her, and hard, watching him sitting next to Lily, stroking her hair as Nurse Jo administered pain medication.

Her parents and other siblings were so far away. If she got hurt or sick no one would be here for her. Her parents couldn't afford to come see her.

There was no one.

No boyfriend, no kids and no family.

*I want that.*

The thought frightened her and she looked away, stepping out of the trauma room. She was just being emotional. It was not part of the plan.

She wanted to bring Bayview Grace to its former glory. That's what she wanted. That was the plan she'd crafted for herself the moment she'd taken her Hippocratic oath.

"Can you page me when Lily Johnson's X-rays come in?" she asked the nurse at the desk.

"Do you want someone from Ortho to handle it, Chief?"

Instead of snapping, Virginia just shook her head and smiled. "No, I'll see to the patient personally. Thanks, Deborah, and this is pro bono. Don't charge them for my services."

The nurse looked stunned, but only for a moment. "Of course, Dr. Potter."

It wasn't often Virginia dealt with minor fractures, let alone wrote off her time, but Lily was a staff member's ward and Gavin had enough to worry about without having to deal with billing. He'd have to fill out the forms, but at least he wouldn't have to deal with his insurance.

"Thank you." Virginia headed back towards her office. She had to put a safe distance between herself and Dr. Brice.

Gavin was fighting hard not to take over the situation. He was after all a trauma surgeon, his life in this hospital was running from room to room and assessing the most serious cases. He wanted to help Lily and it was killing him but he couldn't. He was family and there was a strict rule about physicians and family members.

He'd been shocked to see Virginia come into the room.

It had made his pulse race when she'd walked into the trauma pod, but the woman he'd kissed on the waterfront was gone, replaced by the austere chief of surgery.

And for a moment, when she'd been talking to Lily, she hadn't been that cold professional he'd first met when he'd come to Bayview Grace. For one brief moment he'd seen the woman from this last weekend.

The one he'd kissed.

*Stop thinking about her.*

He had to get her out of his mind. Virginia had made it quite clear what she thought about his kiss when she'd climbed into that cab and left him standing alone on the Embarcadero.

Of course, she'd made it clear to him that she was uncomfortable with the thought of it being a date and he'd promised her it was nothing more than coworkers going out for a quick bite.

And, honestly, that's what he'd thought when he'd shown up at Union Square.

They had just been going out as friends, but as the evening had worn on, he'd been unable to help himself. He was setting himself up to fall for a girl like Virginia.

She was his boss, she was taboo and he was like a moth to her flame. He always liked a challenge, the woman who was hard to get.

He was so rusty, though, when it came to dating women like Virginia. When he'd been traipsing around the world with Border Free Physicians there had been little time for romantic notions. There'd been the odd fling, but that had been all.

Just enough to relieve the itch, and even those had been few and far between.

*This is not part of the plan,* he reminded himself again for the ten thousandth time. He couldn't settle down and bring a strange woman home to the girls. The girls were his life now.

*The girls like Virginia.*

Gavin watched her walk out of the emergency department. Her chestnut hair was in a tight twist again, instead of falling loose over her shoulders. Her white lab coat was crisp, without a crease, the colors she wore were dark, professional, and her black pumps were flawless, without a single scuff.

Even the scent of vanilla was gone from her. Only the antiseptic scent of the hospital burned his nose.

This weekend the Virginia who made his heart race had been soft, both in the colors she'd worn and the scent of her hair.

"I feel funny," Lily said, her eyes wide and a bit dazed.

Nurse Jo chuckled and looked at Gavin. "It's the pain medication."

Gavin smiled and smoothed back the hair from Lily's forehead.

"I can feel my eyeballs, Uncle Gavin. They're round and b-i-g." Lily dragged out the word "big."

Gavin laughed. "It's right about now I should start filming, something to blackmail her with later when she hits those teen years."

"That's about right, Dr. Brice." Jo smiled. The woman had never smiled at him once since he'd started working here. Then again, he'd never really conversed with her before.

"We're ready for her in X-Ray," the orderly said, stepping into the room. "Hey, Dr. Brice."

Gavin nodded to Chet the orderly. "Should I go with her?"

Jo shook her head. "Nope, you know the rules. No family in Radiology. You get to take a seat in the waiting room."

"I'm a doctor here. In fact, I'm head of this department."

Jo crossed her arms. "Are you really going to try and challenge your head nurse, Dr. Brice?"

Gavin held up his hands. "Nope, you're right. I'll just head to the cafeteria. Page me when she gets out of Radiology."

"Will do, Dr. Brice."

Gavin leaned over and pressed a kiss against Lily's forehead. "I'm going to call your grandparents and check on Rose. She was pretty upset when you went to the hospital."

Lily nodded, still wide-eyed.

Gavin had left the room so they could prep Lily for Radiology. He was veering off towards the cafeteria when the charge nurse called after him.

"Paperwork, Dr. Brice. Lots of nice forms for you to fill out."

Gavin groaned. "I'll give you fifty dollars to fill them out for me."

The charge nurse gave him a look that would have made hell freeze over and handed him a clipboard.

"Well, it was worth a shot."

"It was, but no dice, Dr. Brice, and make sure it's legible. I'm *very* familiar with your handwriting."

Gavin rolled his eyes and headed towards the cafeteria, clipboard in hand. He too busy flipping pages and wasn't watching where he was going until he ran smack into a warm, soft body and was spattered with lukewarm coffee.

"Dammit!"

When he glanced up he was standing in front of Virginia, whose crisp white lab coat and blouse were now stained and drenched with coffee.

"Why don't you…?" She trailed off when she realized who it was and her cheeks flushed crimson. "Of course, it had to be you."

# CHAPTER EIGHT

VIRGINIA STEPPED INTO a boardroom as a janitor came to clean up the mess of the two coffees that had just been dumped down her front. Gavin followed her with a roll of paper towels. She could feel the eyes of most of the staff and the patients in the trauma bay boring into the back of her skull. She was absolutely humiliated.

This was the last thing she needed. She peeled off her lab coat and tossed it on the table.

Gavin set down the clipboard beside it and then ripped off a sheet of paper towel, about to mop up the front of her chest.

"I'll take care of that, thanks." She tried not to snap at him, but she was more than annoyed. She had a board meeting later.

"I thought you were heading back to your office."

"I was, until I thought I'd bring you a coffee. You looked like you need a pick-me-up." She dabbed at her shirt, but there was no saving it at the moment. She'd have to change into her scrubs and attend the board meeting like that.

She was sure she'd get comments from some of the snootier members of the board about it.

*Forget about them.*

"It was nice of you to go to the trouble," Gavin said.

"It was no trouble. I was at the coffee cart and thought of you."

Gavin picked up the clipboard and grinned. "So I was an afterthought?"

Virginia sighed impatiently and tossed the soiled paper towel in the garbage. "I told you, you looked a bit pale."

"Well, thanks for the thought."

"You're welcome."

"By the way, I'm not going to be in to work later today." The twinkle in his eyes returned, that mischievous look that she liked so much.

"I assumed that. Your niece happens to be my patient." She eyed the clipboard. "Patient forms?"

Gavin *tsked*. "Yeah, and I've been given dire warnings from the charge nurse about curbing my terrible handwriting."

"Ah, Sara can be a bit of a bull about that. Why don't you fill out the forms here?"

"Only if you keep me company."

"I have a hospital to run," Virginia said. "I have a VIP patient who needs my help."

"She's in Radiology." Gavin pulled out a seat and sat down at the table, beginning to fill in the forms.

"I thought you'd be down in Radiology with her."

"They wouldn't let me. Jo, I think that's her name, can be a bit of a bull when it comes to that."

"Good to know you're learning names."

"Well, someone gave me a hint about name tags."

Virginia chuckled. "Do you want me to talk to them, get them to bend the rules?"

Gavin shook his head. "Nah, I don't want to ruffle any feathers." He cursed under his breath and slammed down his pen.

"What's wrong?" she asked as she pulled another sheet off the roll of paper towels.

"I know none of this information." He dragged his fingers through his hair, making it stand on end. "Dammit."

Gavin stood and stalked toward the far end of the room, muttering and cursing under his breath. She felt sorry for him. Of course he wouldn't have all this information memorized. A mother would, but an uncle who had been thrust into a fatherhood role wouldn't.

"Dammit, what good am I if I can't even remember something simple like her date of birth? Terrible. I shouldn't be doing this."

Virginia closed the boardroom door. "Gavin, what're you talking about?"

"I don't know Lily's birthday!" he snapped, and his hands fisted at his sides. "I know nothing. Everything is at home, in a file, and I've been so damn crazy at work and just trying to get the girls on schedule."

"It's not your fault."

"It is my fault, Virginia. I should know this by now." He cursed again and kicked the wastepaper basket.

Virginia wanted to reach out and hug him, to reassure him that it was okay he didn't know, only she didn't know how. Instead, she picked up the clipboard and began to fill in what she could.

"What're you doing?" he asked.

"Filling out what we can. The rest can come later, we know where you live." Virginia winked at him.

"You don't have to do this."

"It's okay, Gavin. I don't mind."

"Well, maybe I mind."

Virginia set the pen down. She was overstepping her bounds. What right did she have to help him? None. She'd made that clear on Sunday when she'd pushed him away and climbed into that cab.

"I'm sorry," Gavin said, as he scrubbed a hand over his face. "I didn't mean to snap. You were just trying to help."

"It's okay, Gavin." She stood and picked up her soiled lab coat. "Fill in what you can, bring the forms to me and you can phone me with the rest of Lily's information later."

"Don't go. Please stay."

"I have to." Her pager went off and she pulled it out of her coat pocket. "Besides, they're back from Radiology and I have a fracture to assess. Bring the paperwork. Come on."

Gavin nodded and followed her out of the boardroom.

She stopped and realized she needed to change. There was no way she was going to apply a cast to Lily's arm with a coffee-soaked shirt.

"Lily's in room 2121A. I'm going to change and I'll meet you there."

"Sure. See you there." Gavin turned and walked in the other direction towards the ortho wing. Virginia took a deep breath, trying to calm the emotions threatening to overtake her.

And for the first time since meeting Gavin and learning about his situation, she realized that the life he'd fashioned for himself, his plan, had been torn asunder.

Her plan was still sound. She was where she wanted to be. *Am I?*

She shook those thoughts away as she changed in her office bathroom. She put on her green scrubs, replaced everything in the new lab coat and tossed her soiled lab coat in the hospital laundry bag. As for her clothes, she left them in the sink. She'd take them to her dry cleaner's after work.

Janice cocked an eyebrow as she came out of her office in her scrubs.

"What happened to you?" Janice asked.

"Don't ask."

"Did it involve Dr. Brice?"

*What?* Virginia panicked inwardly. "No, why would it?" she asked cautiously.

"The man is a brilliant surgeon, but he's a bit of a klutz. He walks around these halls with his head in the clouds. If you see him barreling towards you, you'd best get out of his way because he won't see you."

"He has a lot on his mind."

Janice's eyebrows arched again in surprise. "You're defending him. Well, this is a first."

Virginia pinched the bridge of her nose. "I have to go put a cast on a little girl. Hold my calls."

"Can't someone from Ortho do that?"

"I can too."

Janice grinned. "I know, but usually minor cases like this you don't bother with. Especially ones involving a child."

Virginia rolled her eyes. "Why are you grinning like that?"

"Because I like this side of you. Could the ice queen be melting?"

Virginia groaned. "Just hold my calls, will you?"

"Of course, Dr. Potter."

Virginia headed off toward the ortho wing, cursing Janice and her uncanny ability to talk about the last thing Virginia wanted to discuss, and that was Dr. Brice. She was sure Janice would interrogate her later about her change of heart when it came to Gavin, because Janice had been listening to Virginia moan and gripe about Gavin since his arrival.

Now she understood him. Gavin wasn't just a faceless jackass, trying to make her life as Chief of Surgery impossible.

She understood where he was coming from, from a certain point of view.

Her life plan was still on track. Gavin's had been derailed.

The first thing Virginia noticed when she entered the room was that Lily wasn't as pale as she'd been before.

"How are we feeling, Lily?" Virginia asked, as the nurse handed her the films.

"Great!" Lily chirped.

Virginia hid her smile as she slid the films onto the light box to study the fracture. "It's just a greenstick fracture. Easy-peasy to fix."

Lily craned her neck to take a look. "Cool, but what do you mean by greenstick?"

"It means your bones are soft and you need to drink more milk," Gavin teased.

Lily rolled her eyes at her uncle. "Do I get a cast?"

"Yes, it's closer to your elbow, so you'll get a fancy cast you'll have to wear for a month."

"Awesome." Lily's eyelids fluttered.

"The pain meds are making her a bit loopy." Gavin rubbed

his eyes. "Damn, I need to call her grandparents. I forgot before. They'll be worried sick."

"Go," Virginia said. "I've got it here."

"Thanks." Gavin left the room and Virginia readied the supplies to make the cast. Lily opened her eyes again.

"Rose is upset."

"I bet she is," Virginia said. "You broke your arm. Was she there when it happened?"

Lily nodded. "She hates hospitals."

"Why?"

"Mom died in one. This one, actually."

Virginia's chest tightened. "I'm sorry to hear that."

"She was worried I was going to die."

"Did she tell you that?" Virginia asked, hopeful Rose only had selective mutism.

"No, but I know what she was thinking when the ambulance came. I was worried too."

Virginia bit back the tears that were threatening to spill. Even though she'd only known these girls for a couple of days, they tugged at her heartstrings. She knew all too well what Rose was feeling for Lily.

Virginia recalled when Shyanne's fallopian tube burst. She'd ridden in the ambulance with her sister, clutching her hand, trying desperately to hold onto Shyanne's life as if life was something tangible you could hold onto.

No matter how hard she'd squeezed, Shyanne had slipped away, like sand through her fingers, bleeding out.

Virginia cleared her throat. "You have a very minor fracture. You'll live, but you're not allowed to hang from the monkey bars again for a while. Now, why don't you tell me what color you want for your cast? I have lots of colors."

"I want pink, please."

"You really have a thing for pink, don't you?" Virginia teased.

Lily grinned. "Pink drives Uncle Gavin bonkers. Personally, I like blue."

"Why do you want to drive your uncle bonkers? I thought you guys loved him."

"Oh, we do, but it's just so funny."

Virginia bit back her chuckle and nodded. "Pink it is."

"Do you have any sisters, Dr. Potter?" Lily asked.

"I do."

"How many?"

Virginia bit her lip and hesitated. "I have two, but I did have three."

"What happened to the third?" Lily's eyes were wide.

"Promise you won't say anything."

"I do," Lily whispered.

"She died."

Lily's face fell. "Were you close?"

Virginia nodded. "Very close. She was my identical twin."

Lily nodded. "I was really close to my mom."

Virginia swallowed the lump in her throat. "I'm sure you were."

"Is your mom still alive, Dr. Potter?"

"Yep, someone has to take care of my other sisters and my two brothers." Well, financially anyway. She hadn't seen them in a long time. It was too hard. Virginia winked and continued finishing up the cast. "There, nice and pink. Do you think that'll drive your uncle bonkers?"

Lily smiled. "Yep."

"Good."


Gavin hung up the phone after his call to the girls' grandparents. They were relieved it was a minor fracture but they were hinting again about taking the girls, about suing for custody again. There were moments when he thought about it, not even bothering to fight it.

Moments like in the boardroom when he didn't even know something as simple as Lily's birth date. He knew generally when it was, he wasn't a total monster, but when Lily had been born he'd been in India.

Then it hit him and he remembered exactly when her birth date was.

*Thank God.*

Joss and Caroline had expressed again what kind of parenting they could provide the girls, but of course halfway around the world, and even then Joss could be transferred somewhere else until he planned to retire from the navy. He had no plans to take a commission in San Francisco.

That was not the life Casey had wanted for her daughters, even though she'd married a military man, they had bought the house outright and she had planned to stay there no matter where her husband was going to be sent.

Casey had been determined she wasn't going to drag her kids from pillar to post.

She'd wanted to give her girls stability.

*"Why did you pick me, Casey?"* he'd asked her. *"I'm not stable. Have someone else take the girls."*

*"You're stable enough for me, Gavin. You took care of me when I was young. Please, I need you to do this for me."*

There was no way he could've said no to Casey. He'd loved her so much, but right now with Lily in hospital, getting a cast on her arm, he felt like he'd let her down. Big time.

Perhaps he should just sign over custody to Joss and Caroline? Maybe that would be for the best.

He didn't know what to do.

He was confused.

He was lost.

Gavin headed back into the room and groaned when he saw what Virginia was doing to Lily's arm, but then he smiled and knew exactly what he was going to do.

There was no way in hell he was going to sign over custody of his nieces. He'd fight the custody issue again and again.

"It had to be pink, huh?"

Virginia grinned as she continued to wrap the cast and Lily shared a secret smile with her that made Gavin instantly suspicious.

"What's going on?" he asked as he took a seat next to Lily.

"Just girl talk," Virginia said absently, but winking at Lily, who giggled.

"If I didn't know better, I'd think you two were conspiring against me or something."

"Oh, please." Virginia snorted. "There, she's all done. I'll write up the discharge papers and you know the drill about cast care."

"Of course," Gavin responded.

"I'll write up a script for pain medication too. Take the rest of the week off, Gavin, if you need to." She turned and left the room.

Gavin knew he should be appreciative that she was willing to give him the rest of the week off, but he wasn't a baby.

"I'll be right back, Lily."

"Okay." Lily closed her eyes and drifted off to sleep, her pink cast propped up.

Gavin chased after Virginia, who was at the charge desk, writing up the papers. "Hey, I don't need the rest of the week off."

Virginia's brow furrowed. "You don't? I thought with Lily…"

"No, she'll be fine with Rosalie. I have a job to do and the girls have to get used to it. Lily's fall wasn't a cry for help or anything."

Virginia's eyes widened, obviously stunned. "I never said it was."

"The implication was there." Gavin's voice rose.

"I really think you should bring your issues up with me later, in private," Virginia whispered.

"I don't need the week off."

Virginia shrugged. "Fine." She pulled the discharge note off the clipboard and handed both it and the script to Gavin. "We'll see you tomorrow. Keep her arm elevated."

Gavin regretted confronting her and he let out a sigh as he watched her walk away. What the hell was wrong with him?

*I'm an idiot.*

With another sigh of regret he folded the note in half and returned to Lily's room to take her home.

# CHAPTER NINE

*I SHOULDN'T BE here. What am I doing here?*

Virginia had been having this argument with herself for the last twenty minutes as she'd sat in her car on the street outside Gavin's home, debating with herself about whether she should ring the doorbell.

This morning he'd been so irrational. Though she really couldn't blame him. He was under a lot of stress.

She was also a bit mad at him for accusing her of thinking Lily had broken her arm on purpose. The child was level-headed and mature, given her age and the fact she'd lost both her parents. Lily had fallen off the monkey bars. Greenstick fractures were the most common fractures in kids.

Heck, she'd sent money last month to her parents because her youngest brother, who was sixteen, had done just the same jumping off the roof of the trailer.

So why was she sitting in her car outside Gavin's house? He was a doctor, he could handle it.

He'd forgotten to fill out his patient forms, at least that's the excuse she'd used to rationalize her appearance outside his house.

Really, she need to get her clothes to the dry cleaner's, have some dinner and get to bed early because she'd managed to reschedule the board meeting until tomorrow.

But, no, she was sitting in her car, mentally arguing with herself.

When had life become so complicated?

*The moment I hired Dr. Gavin Brice.*

With a sigh she got out of the car and headed towards the door. The gate was locked so she rang the bell. The moment the bell rang, the curtains twitched and she saw little Rose standing in the living-room window in her pajamas.

Virginia smiled and waved and Rose waved back before disappearing, just as the door opened. Gavin opened the door in a ratty old T-shirt and pajama pants. There were dark circles under his eyes and his hair was sticking up on end.

"Dr. Potter?"

"I didn't wake you up, did I?" She glanced at her wristwatch. It was only seven o'clock in the evening.

"Yes, but it's okay. I must've dozed off during the movie." He unlocked the gate. "Come on in."

"No, it's okay. I just brought the patient forms. You forgot to fill them out and both our asses are on the line from Jo and my assistant Janice."

"Thanks." He took the forms and his gaze roved her from head to toe. "You're still in your scrubs?"

"Well, my street clothes are still covered with coffee."

Gavin chuckled and rubbed the back of his neck. "Again, sorry."

"I'll be going." She turned to leave, but he grabbed her arm.

"Come in for a few minutes and check on your VIP patient."

"I don't think that's wise, do you?"

"As friends. I promise, nothing else will happen. Scout's honor."

"I don't know, Gavin."

"Look, don't make me stand out here in these ridiculous PJs any longer. I don't want my neighbors talking. Come in and say hi to the girls. Lily hasn't stopped yammering about her visit with you today and I think Rose is a bit jealous."

"Okay, for a few moments." Virginia stepped inside and Gavin locked up. "So why are PJs so ridiculous? They look quite comfortable to me."

"I sleep nude." He winked and headed up the stairs.

*I had to ask.* Heat flushed her cheeks and she tried not to picture Gavin naked, though she'd done that very thing since Sunday, when he'd kissed her and she'd almost forgotten who she'd been kissing.

She squished something rubbery under her feet and Rose materialized again at the top of the stairs, arms crossed and giving them the look of death.

Gavin rolled his eyes and scooped down to retrieve the rubber giraffe out from under her feet, yet again. "Rose, you have to stop setting booby traps on the steps. Here, take Georgiana and stop subjecting her to such horrible torture."

Rose caught her giraffe and rolled her eyes as if to say *puhleze* and walked away.

"She's got a thing about that giraffe on the steps."

Gavin groaned. "Every time I go out. I swear that damn giraffe wasn't on the steps when I went down."

Virginia chuckled. "It's okay."

When she walked into the living room she noticed Lily in the corner of the sectional sofa, propped up with pillows.

"Dr. Potter, what're you doing here?" Lily asked, but her voice betrayed her joy, which made Virginia's heart squeeze with pleasure.

*Don't get attached.*

"I've come to sign your cast. I forgot to do that before."

Lily beamed. "Sure!"

Virginia pulled a marker out of her purse and sat down next to Lily. She signed her name and drew a small cartoon frog. "There, now it's officially one of my casts. I always have to sign the casts I make. It's a rule."

"Thanks!"

Rose was frowning and Virginia could see a look of envy on her face. "Do you have a bear that needs a cast?"

Rose nodded and took off towards the back of the house.

"What're you doing?" Gavin asked.

"Saving you another trip to the hospital."

Rose reappeared with a bear and Virginia pulled out a roll of pink tape. "I presume pink, yes?"

Rose nodded vehemently and Virginia proceeded to apply a cast to her teddy's arm. When she was done, she signed the teddy's cast and drew the same goofy frog on it. "Now, make sure his cast doesn't get wet, keep his arm elevated and I'll see him in a month to get it removed."

Rose nodded solemnly and headed back to her bedroom.

"Nice move, Dr. Potter." Gavin grinned.

"Thanks." She put her pen away and stood up. "I should head for home. Long day of meetings tomorrow and I don't want to interrupt your…"

"We're having a sleepover pajama party tonight in the living room. Though we're not going to get to do manicures." Lily pouted for a brief moment and turned her attention back to the television.

Virginia cocked an eyebrow and eyed Gavin. "A sleepover. You're such a good uncle."

Gavin shrugged. "I try. I'm hoping her painkillers will kick in soon and I can carry them both back to bed."

Rose stormed back into the living room, wearing her pink tutu and curled up close to Lily. Virginia noticed it was really close, like Rose didn't want to let Lily out of sight for longer than she had to. Virginia knew how Rose felt. She missed Shyanne with every fiber of her being.

"Is Rose okay?" Virginia whispered.

"Yeah, I think she misses her grandparents. She was clingy when they went to the airport this afternoon." Gavin shrugged again.

Virginia glanced at the little girl in time to see an eye-roll and shaking her head in disagreement. "You think so?"

Virginia didn't think it was the grandparents' absence.

"What else can it be?"

Virginia pulled him into the hallway out of earshot. "Lily mentioned your sister passed away at Bayview Grace."

Gavin's expression softened and he scrubbed his hand over

his face. "Yeah, oh, hell. I didn't even think of that. Damn, and I go there every day to work. I never even thought of it. I started working there after Casey died."

Now it was Virginia's turn to feel guilty. She'd had no idea when she'd first hired Gavin that his sister had been an oncology patient and that she'd died in the hospital.

*I'm the worst boss ever.*

*But, then, how could she have known? Gavin was such a private man.*

"Gavin, I'm so sorry that I didn't know."

"No one knew, Virginia. I didn't want anyone's pity or condolences. I just needed the job. You know how I feel about the bureaucracy of my position."

Virginia nodded. "Still, if I had known…"

"Let's not talk about it. I'll mention this incident to Rose's counselor. Just another thing to add to the plate."

Virginia bit her lip and set her purse down on the hall table. "Why don't you have a shower or do something you like to do by yourself and I'll sit with the girls for a while? I'll give Lily and Rose a manicure, a nice-looking lacquer job."

"You don't have to do that. You have a busy day tomorrow."

"I insist. Besides, I'm not the only one. You took an unexpected day off and there was no head of trauma there to wrestle some of those residents in."

Gavin groaned and smiled. "Fine. I think I'll go have a shower or something. Thanks."

"No problem. Just bring me some nice pink nail polish."

He groaned. "Always with the pink."

Virginia laughed and headed back into the living room. The girls were watching a cartoon movie, something really annoying with terrible music.

"How about something a bit more fun? Something we can sing to? What movies do you have?"

"Mom's old DVDs are on the shelf there."

Virginia wandered over to the shelf and searched the titles, hoping Casey had had the DVD she was thinking of, and she almost shouted for joy when she pulled *The Sound of Music* out of the stack.

"Have you guys seen this movie?"

Lily and Rose shook their heads. "Isn't that Mary Poppins?" Lily asked.

Virginia grinned. "Yes, but this movie is awesome to sing to. I love singing to it. Whenever I was sick I would watch this movie over and over again."

She and Shyanne would sing the soundtrack at the top of their lungs. The last time she'd watched it had been a long time ago, with Shyanne right before she'd died. *The Sound of Music*, *Grease* and *Oklahoma!* to name a few had helped her while away many hours on the couch when she'd been feeling under the weather. It had also helped to drown out the sound of her parents fighting over money.

To this day, whenever she was feeling a bit rundown she'd pop on one of these old musicals and she'd feel like she was at home and comforted.

Julie Andrews had been more of a mother to her than her own mother had.

Gavin wandered in with the nail polish and, surprisingly, nail-polish remover, which caused Lily to squeal and Rose to jump up and down excitedly, because they knew what was about to happen.

He excused himself and Virginia put on the movie.

When the first number started Virginia took a seat between the two girls and started on Rose's nails first.

Gavin could hear the strains of the movie soundtrack drifting from upstairs. He retreated to the small basement and did some weights. Whenever he was stressed, he would work out. When he'd been traveling all over the world, working out had usually meant playing soccer, cricket or running. Exercising gave him the rush of endorphins he needed to put everything into perspective and he was still stressed about his run-in with the girls' grandparents when he'd brought Lily home.

They'd made it clear to him in no uncertain terms that they were going to petition for full custody of the girls.

Their reasoning was that he was a single man with no clue on how to be a proper father and they were the girls' grand-parents, the closest the girls had to real parents.

He liked Joss and Caroline, but they had their faults.

Where had they been when Casey had been dying? Where had they been when Casey had been trying to fight the cancer that had claimed her life? When she'd been dragging herself to chemo appointments and raising two little girls on her own?

Then again, where had he been? He hadn't come back to the States until she'd called him to tell him she was dying.

Casey had been raising the girls on her own since Rose's birth and it broke Gavin's heart that he'd been halfway around the world, letting his sister fend for herself.

Joss and Caroline hadn't been there either.

When Casey had been dying they hadn't given up their lives, Joss hadn't retired from the service or tried to get a commis-sion in San Francisco. No, but he had given up everything to be a father to these girls and he was damn well going to re-main that way.

He'd fight Joss and Caroline tooth and nail to keep the girls.

Gavin continued to lift weights until he was exhausted and the sweat was pouring down his body.

After this he'd need to take another cold shower, because he couldn't get Virginia out of his mind.

He couldn't remember ever obsessing over one woman so much, but then again any woman he'd pursued for a brief dal-liance hadn't brushed him aside and neither had he ever pur-sued his boss before.

Not that he'd really had a boss like Virginia before.

For a moment he fantasized that they were alone, that they weren't colleagues and were just two people who were attracted to each other. Two people who wanted one another and could give in to that passion.

He couldn't help but wonder what it would be like to take

Virginia in his arms and make love to her. She was so prim and proper, but when he'd kissed her she'd melted just a bit and he couldn't help but wonder if she'd ignite under his touch.

*Get a hold of yourself.*

He was definitely going to need a cold shower and soon. First he had to get his mind off of her before he went upstairs in his current state, which was a hard thing to do, given the fact she was under the same roof as him.

When he set down the weights he realized the television had gone strangely quiet and he glanced at the wall and balked when he saw that it was close to midnight.

He'd let time get away from him.

He toweled himself off and headed back upstairs half-dressed. Everything was silent when he headed toward the living room.

"Virginia—" Gavin stopped when he noticed that Virginia was curled up on the couch, Rose was lying beside her and Lily was snoring in the corner.

The television was on, but the DVD was frozen on the scene selection menu. She looked so peaceful. They all did.

It surprised to him to see Virginia curled up with the girls, but it also pleased him. The girls' nails were the color of bubblegum and then he noticed Virginia's neat, well-manicured nails were also the color of bubblegum, and it wasn't a very tidy job.

Which meant she'd let one of the girls do it.

A smile tugged at the corner of his mouth. She was so tender, so beautiful.

*Don't think about her like that. She doesn't want you.*

Virginia had made it clear. Nothing could ever happen between them.

He moved to wake her up and then thought better of it. Virginia was exhausted; there were dark circles under her eyes. She'd had a pretty trying day herself.

Instead he shut the television off and then picked up the afghan from the recliner and tucked all the girls in.

Only two of them were his.

And the other one he wanted desperately to be his too.

The incessant squeaking in Virginia's ear alerted her to the fact she wasn't in her apartment. She cracked open one eye to see a silent golden angel holding a rubber giraffe by the name of Georgiana in her face.

Rose gave it another long squeak, which sent shooting pain up Virginia's neck and behind her eyeballs. Then she realized she'd spent the night on Gavin's couch. She bolted upright.

"Oh, my God."

Rose wagged her finger and squeaked Georgiana again.

"Sorry, I didn't mean to curse." She glanced around the room until she spied the clock and realized she was going to be late for the board meeting.

*Crap.*

"I have to get to work." She stood up and realized she was still in the same scrubs she'd worn the previous day.

*Double crap.*

"Good morning," Gavin said, as he came into the room. He was dressed for work, coffee in his hand, and by the way his hair was glistening he'd obviously had a shower.

"Why didn't you wake me up last night?"

"You looked so peaceful."

Virginia groaned. "You should've woken me up. I need a shower and a change of clothes. I have an important meeting in an hour."

"There are some of Casey's clothes in the master bedroom and you can always borrow my shower."

"I don't think that would be appropriate."

Gavin took a sip out of his travel mug. "What's not appropriate about offering a friend some spare clothes and a shower?"

*He had a point.*

It wasn't ideal, but she really didn't have a choice. She hadn't become Chief of Surgery by attending meetings dressed as a slob.

"Point me in the right direction."

"Gladly."

She followed Gavin to the master bedroom. The room smelled distinctly like him. Masculine. A clean, spicy smell that she loved. The bed was made and she noticed a pile of blankets on the floor.

"What's going on here?" she asked as she stepped over the pile.

"Ah, I'm still not used to using a mattress. I've been sleeping rough for so long I find I can only get a good night's sleep on the floor."

"You've been in San Francisco for how long again?"

"Six months, but still no good. The bed is too soft and good for only one thing."

Virginia's pulse began to race, understanding his implication clearly.

"Clothes?" she asked, changing the subject.

He moved past her and opened up the closet. "Here's where Casey's clothes are."

"Why are you still keeping them?"

Gavin shrugged. "I haven't had the time to deal with her personal effects. Besides, they come in handy when I deliberately trap women here and force them to babysit my nieces."

Virginia rolled her eyes and snorted.

He opened another door. "There are towels in the closet. Feel free to use whatever."

"Thanks. I really appreciate this. I'll see you at work."

Gavin nodded. "See you."

When he left the bedroom Virginia peeled off the scrubs and climbed into the shower. The hot water helped work out the kinks in her back and neck.

She finished her quick shower and then dried herself off, towel-drying her hair. As much as she wished she had a straightener or a blow-dryer, she was just thankful she didn't smell like plaster or old coffee.

When she headed into the master bedroom she picked out

a simple blouse and pants, which were a little big on her but at least she wouldn't be in wrinkled old scrubs. She jammed the scrubs in her purse after tying back her hair.

As soon as she left the bedroom Gavin was standing there, holding a mug of coffee out.

"Please, don't dump that on me."

"You might want me to." He winced. "Your car was parked in a no overnight parking zone and was towed."

Virginia closed her eyes and took a deep calming breath. What she really wanted to do was let out a string of profanities that would shake the very rafters of Gavin's pink home, but there were children in the house, so she refrained from uttering them out loud and kept them to herself.

"How am I going to get to work?" she asked calmly.

"You can ride with me, but I hope you don't mind riding on the back of my bike. Rosalie needs the van for the girls today."

"You ride a motorcycle?"

He nodded. "I do. What do you say, Virginia?"

Her heart beat a bit faster in anticipation at the thought of riding behind the most stereotypical bad boy. She did have a thing for motorcycles.

Instead of saying *I'd love that* and letting him know how exciting the prospect was, she restrained herself. "Sure, I really don't have a choice."

"Don't sound so enthused," he teased. "Well, let's go."

Virginia downed the rest of her coffee and followed Gavin outside to the garage. He uncovered the Harley and dug out an extra helmet for her. She was really excited to ride behind him, but she also hoped no one from the hospital would see her arrive on the back of Gavin's motorcycle.

The gossip would be endless and she didn't want anything to get back to the board about it. It could put her career and Gavin's in jeopardy.

He secured her purse and his satchel in one of the panniers, before climbing on.

She climbed on the back of his motorcycle and wrapped

her arms around him. The moment she did so, her heart beat a bit faster and she hoped he didn't notice. What she really longed to do was press her body tight against his, but she kept her distance the best she could. Still, it felt so good to be so close to him.

"Hold on." He revved the engine and the purr of the bike drowned out the loud beat of her pulse. The vibrations rippled through her. He pulled out onto the street, parked and shut the garage door before climbing back on. "You ready?"

Virginia nodded and he turned on his signal and hit the streets of San Francisco. The moment he hit the road, she pulled him tighter as she held on for dear life. She'd lived in San Francisco for years, she learned to drive on its streets when she'd first moved here and had ridden the streetcars and trolleys up and down the hills, but until now those hills had never freaked her out.

She repressed the urge to cry out as Gavin maneuvered his way through the San Francisco streets towards Bayview Grace.

The ride terrified her, but it also thrilled her. As they crested a hill and raced down the other side she felt like she was on some crazy roller coaster.

For the first time in a long time she felt carefree and that feeling scared her. When they arrived at Bayview Grace Gavin parked in his reserved spot.

"What did you think of the ride?" he asked as she handed him her helmet.

Her knees wobbled a bit. "It was… Thanks for bringing me."

Gavin grinned. "Any time. If you want, I'll take you to the lot to retrieve your car after work."

"No, thanks, Dr. Brice. I'll take transit or a cab. I'm not sure how late I'll be working tonight."

"Sure. Thanks again for your help with the girls last night."

"My pleasure." She glanced at her watch and saw she was already five minutes late. "Look, I have to go. Thanks."

What she wanted to say was that it was no problem and that she would gladly spend another evening with the girls.

She also wanted to tell him how much she'd enjoyed the impromptu sleepover party with them and how good it had felt to have two sweet little angels sleeping next to her on the couch, but she didn't.

It wasn't her place.

She turned on her heel and walked briskly towards the hospital. Her legs were still shaking from the ride and her heart was shaking a bit from the feelings that were threatening to overpower her common sense.

# CHAPTER TEN

WHEN VIRGINIA CAME out of the board meeting a few hours later, she had a pounding headache. Janice was waiting for her in her office with some files.

"You look like you've been run over by a steamroller," she remarked.

"Haven't I?" Virginia asked as she took a seat behind her desk. "More budget cuts."

"Ugh," Janice remarked.

"My sentiments exactly."

Virginia was frustrated. The board had hired her to bring this hospital back from the dead, but how was she supposed to do that when they constantly cut her budget?

Because they wanted a private clinic, at least some of them did, and she wasn't going to let go of her ER without a fight. So she'd proposed a hospital benefit. A glitzy affair showcasing their brilliant attendings and the innovative strides they were making in order to receive funding.

Her suggestion had pleased the board no end, but it meant she had a big party to plan. So instead of spending time with patients, doing innovative surgeries or research she was going to be planning a big party.

"That's an interesting color choice and I don't mean to be disrespectful, but who did your nails?"

Virginia glanced down at her hands and groaned inwardly. Rose had painted her nails, and they were horribly mangled, messy and now the enamel was chipping. It was also pink. No wonder she had been getting weird glances from some of the members of the board.

"I'm not on the top of my game today."

Janice cocked an eyebrow. "No kidding. Wild night last night?" There was a hint of hope in her assistant's voice. Janice was always hoping that Virginia would live a little and she voiced her opinions quite loudly at times.

*"You're young. Don't spend your youth locked away. Go out and live a little."*

Why couldn't they just let her be? It was her life after all.

She knew one thing: planning benefits and schmoozing hadn't been part of the original plan. Virginia wanted to be in the OR or researching.

The internal dialog in her head was turning into a bit of a broken record.

"Well, what were you up to last night?" Janice prodded.

"A bit of an impromptu sleepover." She groaned inwardly, regretting the admission, because when Janice got a hint of gossip, she was like a dog with a bone. Virginia was usually more aloof with Janice, but lack of a good night's sleep had caused a lapse in judgement and she'd let down her walls a bit.

"Oh, do tell." Janice was grinning from ear to ear.

"You know, it's funny. I have all this work to do."

Janice snorted and dropped the last file on her desk. "Fine, I can take a hint. Before I go, though, A&B Towing called and they had information on where your car is being held. The message is the pink slip on the top."

Janice shot her a knowing but smug look as she left the office.

Virginia groaned. She'd forgotten about her car. She only had an hour before the impound lot closed. Her paperwork could wait until she got back. She needed her car.

When she left her office, Janice was smiling secretly to herself as she worked. Virginia just shook her head and left for the lot.

* * *

"I heard you were looking for this." Gavin dropped the patient forms onto Janice's desk. He'd meant to drop them off sooner, but he'd had a surgery to attend. He'd literally just got out of the OR. All he'd had time to do was scrub out, and he was still wearing his scrub cap, because Janice had been paging him about the missing forms since he'd arrived.

"Thank you, Dr. Brice, and very neat handwriting too."

"Sorry I didn't drop them off straightaway."

Janice cocked an eyebrow and looked at him over her horned-rimmed glasses. "Well, I can be persistent when I need something done. I know how distracted you surgeons get."

Gavin lingered and he didn't know why.

*You know why.*

"Is Dr. Potter out of her meeting yet?"

Janice's eyes widened and then she grinned and leaned forward. "Yes, but she had to step out. Her car was impounded last night. So unlike Dr. Potter."

"Right. I forgot."

"Really? You knew about her car being impounded? Do tell." Janice leaned on her elbow, propping her chin on her fist and fluttering her eyelashes behind her tortoiseshell bifocals.

Gavin held up his hands. "I don't think it's any of my business to tell you. If Virginia didn't mention it, then I won't."

"Virginia? Usually other surgeons refer to her as Dr. Potter or chief. Didn't realize you two were so close." Janice grinned like the cat that had got the cream, or like the Grinch when he thought of his evil plan. So smugly pleased with herself.

Gavin cursed inwardly. "You're a bit of a pest, aren't you?"

"One of the best, Dr. Brice."

Gavin backed away. He didn't want to make Virginia angrier at him. "Well, I'm being paged. I'd better go."

Janice gave him a skeptical look. "Of course, Dr. Brice. Of course."

Gavin made a mental note not to cross swords with Janice, though some of the nurses had already warned him of that.

Janice was a force to be reckoned with. She'd been a charge nurse herself for years and was the keeper of the gates, more intimidating than Cerberus itself. Although it was Gavin's experience that women like Janice had barks that were worse than their bites. She had implied that there was something personal between himself and Virginia.

Though he wanted something more intimate, he knew if he went after Virginia it wouldn't be just a fling and he wasn't sure if he had anything to give Virginia because marriage and monogamy were something he had never pictured for himself.

When he headed back down to the trauma bay Dr. Rogerson popped out of a room.

Gavin liked independent, strong woman, but he didn't like being hunted down by overly forward women. To Moira Rogerson he was just a piece of meat and he didn't like it.

"How's your niece, Dr. Brice?"

Gavin frowned. "How did you know?"

He liked to keep his personal life just that—to himself. Especially with people he worked with.

"I was on duty yesterday. I was originally paged until the ice queen took over."

Gavin didn't like that nickname, knowing that was the name the other surgeons used when referring to Virginia. Ice Queen was far from the truth.

She might be a bit heavy-handed when it came to running the hospital, but Virginia wasn't that way outside work. He'd seen the softer side of her.

"Well, Dr. Potter is a trauma surgeon and my niece broke her arm." Gavin pulled out his phone and pretended to check for text messages, though he had none. Moira didn't get the hint that he wasn't interested in talking.

"I didn't know you were guardian to your nieces. That's really sweet." Moira grinned at him, a smile meant to devour a man whole.

"I don't talk much about them. I like to keep my private life private."

He walked into the lunchroom and got himself a drink of water. Moira followed him and he groaned inwardly, wishing she would just go away.

"How old are your nieces?"

Swallowing the water was like trying to down a cue ball at the moment. "Why do you want to know?"

"Just trying to make small talk." Moira took a step forward and placed her hand on his arm, gently squeezing it.

"I'm afraid I don't do small talk."

Moira smiled. "What do you do, then?"

"Surgery?" he offered, and Moira just laughed, which was annoying and high-pitched, and she clutched his arm tighter.

"You're so droll, Gavin."

He ground his teeth, not liking the way she said his name. "I don't know what's so funny about stating the truth."

"So would you like to have dinner sometime? Maybe tonight?"

Gavin was about to answer and glanced up in time to see Virginia walk back into the hospital. His heart skipped a beat as he watched her walk through the entrance and he was taken back to that stolen moment on Sunday, down by the water, when time had seemed to stand still and he'd pulled Virginia into his arms and kissed her.

The scent of her perfume, the touch of her lips still burned in his memory, as did the pointed rejection, which still stung him.

Virginia and he were coworkers, maybe even friends, but that's all they could be.

She'd made that pretty clear.

"Gavin?" Moira turned to see what had caught his attention. "Oh, the ice queen."

"Sure, why don't we go out tonight?" Gavin suddenly blurted out, trying not to look at Virginia as she headed towards them.

Moira grinned. "Yes, I'd love that. I'll page you later for the details." Moira winked and finally left him in peace.

Virginia nodded curtly to Moira as they passed in the hall

and then, as if knowing she was being watched, she glanced at him. Her dark gaze locked with his and he saw a faint pinkness tinge her skin as she walked into the room.

"You're still here. I thought your shift ended a couple of hours ago?" she said.

"Surgery. The closest hospital was packed and the ambulance rerouted here."

A brief smile flitted on her lips and he knew it wasn't because of the possibility that someone had been injured. Virginia was thinking in terms of business for Bayview Grace.

"I'm glad the ambulance thought to reroute here."

"We were the closest and the man was in no condition to wait for the ambulance to take him to the level two trauma. I don't think that's something we should be celebrating."

Virginia bit her bottom lip and gave him a quizzical look. "I'm not celebrating."

"Come on, I saw the brief smile that flitted across your face."

She pinched the bridge of her nose and sighed. He knew that response and he'd come to loathe it, especially after she'd had a meeting with the board of directors.

He moved past her and shut the door to the room then pulled the blinds to the room so they were in relative privacy.

"What's going on?"

Virginia shrugged her shoulders. "I don't know what you mean."

"I know that look. Very well."

This time she did smile and her shoulders relaxed from the tense hunch they'd had just moments before.

"It was just a long day and I didn't get the best sleep last night."

"What're you talking about? That couch is too soft."

Virginia cocked an eyebrow. "Says the man who sleeps on the hardwood floor."

"Did the meeting have something to do with me?" he asked. "You can tell me. I know for a fact you can tell me."

The smile disappeared and she sighed again. "Not you directly, just in general financial terms."

"That bad?"

"I have to organize a benefit for the end of the month. A real glitzy affair." She wrinkled her nose in disgust. "Not my most favorite job."

"I don't blame you." He rubbed the back of his neck. "Black tie, I suppose?"

"Yes, and mandatory for all Attendings. One month from today, so get yourself a sitter."

"Ugh."

Virginia chuckled and opened the door. "My sentiments exactly. Are you headed for home now?"

"I think so. I just dropped those forms off to Janice."

"Good."

They walked out of the room together.

"Hey, if you need help planning the gala or benefit, whatever you want to call it, just ask."

"You have hidden depths, Dr. Brice. I thought you were a roughneck sort of physician?"

"That may be, but I've attended many, many, many mandatory galas on behalf of Border Free Physicians."

"Well, maybe I'll take you up on your offer. I hate party planning. I never had a party when I was young."

"Never had a party?" Gavin asked, intrigued by this insight into her.

"No, my parents couldn't stretch to that luxury."

"What did they do?"

"Unemployed, for the most part. I grew up in a trailer in South Dakota with two brothers and three sisters."

"That's a surprise."

"Really? Why do you say that?"

"You don't seem the trailer type."

Virginia crossed her arms. "Is there a trailer type?"

Gavin rubbed the back of his neck. "Sorry, no, there isn't

unless you count what's on television. I didn't mean to make assumptions."

"It's okay. I have hidden depths. Ugh, I hope someone can help."

"A surgeon as a party planner?" Gavin asked in disbelief. "Surgeons usually aren't social types."

"You'd be surprised around here." Virginia tucked a way-ward lock of brown hair behind her ear. "I saw you talking to Dr. Rogerson. She's a bit of a social butterfly."

*Is she jealous?*

Gavin was amused, pleased she'd noticed, but he didn't want to talk about it. He'd let her stew a bit. "Well, I'd better head for home. The girls get anxious when I'm late."

"Of course. Have a good evening and send them my best." Virginia turned and walked away from him towards the office.

Gavin watched her walk away.

And then a horrible thought crept into his mind. If the hospital needed to throw a benefit, one that would cause the chief of surgery a large amount of stress, how bad a shape was the hospital in and would he even have a job in the near future?

# CHAPTER ELEVEN

GAVIN MANAGED TO finagle Rosalie into babysitting. He owed that woman a large Christmas bonus.

Now he was standing in the middle of Union Square, waiting for Moira to arrive. He glanced over and saw the place where Virginia had been waiting for him. When he'd seen her there, he'd been mesmerized by her simple beauty and he'd known he'd have a hard time keeping his hands off her.

Virginia occupied his mind constantly, made him think things he shouldn't.

Was that why he'd agreed on this date with Moira and suggested this location, re-creating the date he and Virginia had gone on? Was he trying to prove to himself that he could find that spark with anyone, that Virginia wasn't special?

He didn't have time to contemplate it further as Moira walked over to him. She was dressed nicely, different from her scrubs. She was dressed as prettily as Virginia, only the color was a deep emerald, which suited Moira's hair. It was also more seductive and instead of ballet flats she wore heels, which were impractical for the date he had in mind. Of course, Moira wasn't to know that.

"Hi," she said, her smile bright as she stopped in front of him. She leaned over and gave him a peck on the cheek. Her perfume was a bit overpowering and floral. Not homey like vanilla and certainly not subtle.

"Hi, yourself."

"Where are we going? I hope it's not far." Moira pointed to her heels and then lifted the hem of her dress slightly, showing off her leg. "These are murder on my feet, but they're so pretty."

"I was actually thinking of the Fog City Diner."

"Oh." There was a hint of disappointment in her voice.

Gavin didn't know what she'd expected. Obviously something fancier as she was decked out to the nines.

"Is there something wrong with that restaurant? I've been told it's a San Francisco institution."

"For tourists, yes."

"I made reservations."

"Sounds good." Gavin could tell she was lying by the way she forced a smile. "Is your car nearby? I took a cab here as mine's in the shop."

"No, I'd thought we'd take the streetcar."

"You're kidding me, right?"

*I guess I am.* "No, I'm not kidding. I thought we'd take the streetcar and enjoy the sights."

"How about I pay for a cab? No offense, but these heels are a little much for a streetcar."

"Sure." What could he say to that, no? Gavin trailed behind Moira as she marched over to a taxi stand at a nearby hotel. It didn't take long before they were both settled into the back of the cab. Moira snuggled up next to him, her floral scent mixed with the spicy smell permeating the cab, making his stomach turn.

Virginia had had no problem riding the streetcar. In fact, it had seemed to enhance the experience of that night. It had been fun. Virginia wasn't high-maintenance. He had an inkling, going into this date, that Moira was high-maintenance.

Did he really want to date someone who was?

This wasn't for the long term, he reminded himself again. This was just a fling. Who cared if Moira preferred different things to Virginia? This wasn't a comparison between the two women. He wasn't looking for something long term.

Though maybe he was and that thought scared him.

On that short cab ride to the Fog City Diner, Gavin finally admitted to himself how lonely he'd been and maybe he did want to settle down and have it all. The thought was extremely unsettling. Having custody of the girls had changed his perspective entirely.

The conversation at the diner was one-sided and stilted. Moira chatted away, but Gavin just couldn't clear his head from his jangled thoughts. It'd been so easy to talk to Virginia.

"Gavin, are you listening?"

"Sorry, what?"

Moira frowned. "You're a bit out of sorts."

"A bit. What were you saying?"

"I was just telling you how some staff members think the ice queen is melting. That her demeanor is softening around her cold, hard exterior. Can you imagine? I wonder what brought that on, though I have my suspicions."

"Softening? How do you mean?"

"Well, she's been behaving differently lately. I think it's a man."

Gavin's heart stuttered, but then he shrugged, feigning indifference. "Maybe she has a lot on her mind."

"Who knows? But she's been more…I don't know…approachable. More relaxed and nice. Not so aloof. The nurses like the change."

"I don't quite see the problem, then."

Moira leaned forward. "I've heard talk of the ER getting the axe."

Now she had Gavin's full attention. He'd been sure something was up with Virginia planning that gala.

"Who told you that?"

Moira grinned. "Ah, so you've heard it too."

"Nothing concrete, just rumors. Especially rumors involving a certain fundraising event."

"The gala! Yeah, it had me worried too. My source is on the board of directors."

Gavin cocked an eyebrow. "Go on."

"There are threats to close the ER, but Dr. Potter is fighting tooth and nail to keep it open."

Gavin grinned, pleased to hear it. They called Virginia the ice queen. How little they knew when she was working so hard for them and they had no idea. "Is she?"

Moira sighed. "It won't do her any good. It's why I applied to another hospital and got a job."

"You're leaving Bayview?"

"Before it sinks. I have to protect myself and my career. If you're nice to me I can get you an interview." She slid her hand across the table, reaching out for his, and then her foot began to slide up his leg in a very suggestive manner. A move he would've welcomed six months ago.

"I think your thoughts on Bayview sinking are premature. I think Dr. Potter will save Bayview Grace."

Moira frowned, retracting her hand, and the game of footsie ended as well. "Why did you say yes to this date, Gavin?"

"What do you mean?"

She rolled her eyes. With a sigh she opened her purse and placed a twenty on the table. "You're clearly not interested in me. You're obviously hung up on someone else. I don't want to spend my evening talking hospital politics."

She slid out of the booth and stood. Gavin panicked and jumped in front of her, grabbing her by the shoulders and pulling her close to him before crushing her lips against his in a kiss. A kiss to prove to himself and her that he wasn't hung up on anyone.

Moira melted into his arms, a moan escaping from the back of her throat, then her tongue pushed past his lips.

Gavin felt nothing.

His kiss with Virginia had been so different. It had been gentle, sweet and it'd turned him on. This was rough, clumsy and evoked no response from him at all.

He didn't want Moira. He wanted Virginia.

Moira broke the kiss. She sighed and then frowned. "Goodbye, Dr. Brice."

Gavin didn't try to stop her this time as she walked past curious onlookers as she left the restaurant. He sank back down against the seat, before pulling out a couple of twenties to pay the bill.

When he walked outside a thick fog was rolling in and the sun was just starting to get ready to set, making the area glow orange in the haze. Gavin walked along the Embarcadero. August would soon be over. The girls would go back to school. He had to switch to nights so he could take them to and from school. Rosalie already said she'd take them during the nights he worked.

There would be no time for dating.

Not until the girls were older.

Only would it make a difference? Would he even have a job in a few weeks' time?

Was Moira doing the smart thing by jumping ship?

Gavin didn't know how long he walked, but he ended up in front of Bayview Grace. Virginia's car was still in the lot.

*I need to know.*

He had two little girls depending on him. He needed job security and stability in order to keep the girls. If he lost his job and had to move, the girls' grandparents would certainly sue for custody and possibly win. It would kill him to lose the girls now.

Virginia shuffled through more paperwork and glanced at the clock. It was almost eight. She should really go home, but what would she be going home to?

Nothing.

Then her mind wandered to Gavin. She knew he was on a date with Moira Rogerson. She'd heard it through the rumor mill—well, she'd actually heard it from Janice, who kept an ear to the grapevine.

It shouldn't bother her because she wasn't looking for a relationship, but it did. It made her feel jealous, just picturing him laughing and talking with Moira like he'd done with her.

If he started dating Moira she had no one to blame but herself. She'd pushed him away and it was for the best. She couldn't give him what he wanted because she was terrified to admit it was what she wanted as well, but she wouldn't put her heart at risk again.

She wouldn't lose anyone else she loved.

Virginia sighed and set down her papers. She stood up and stretched, deciding it was time to leave when the door to her office burst open. Virginia jumped and saw Gavin standing there, dressed in the same kind of clothes he'd worn when he'd taken her out.

"Dr. Brice, I thought you were out for the evening."

"I was, but I needed to talk to you."

The butterflies in her stomach began to flutter. "Oh?"

"I need to… I mean, I want…" Gavin rubbed the back of his neck and then shut the door behind him. "I need to switch to nights."

"Oh—oh, okay." Virginia took a seat, her knees knocking. She didn't know what she'd been expecting him to say, but it definitely wasn't that. She felt relieved and disappointed all at the same time. "Why?"

"The girls start school the first week of September and I want to be able to take them to and from school. It's Rose's first year there and I think it's important that I'm there."

Virginia nodded. "Of course. I would ask if you've talked to your superior but as you're head of that department there shouldn't be a problem. I'm sure someone will want to change."

"Jefferson is switching with me. He's young and he's looking forward to day shifts, even if it's only for the school year."

"Then it's all settled." Virginia watched him. He looked nervous and he stood there as if he wanted to say more. "Is that all you needed to talk about, Gavin?"

"No." His gaze met hers, those deep green eyes intense, riveting her to the spot. "Is the ER threatened?"

Virginia cleared her throat. "What're you talking about?"

"The gala. It's not just some fundraiser, it's to save the ER, isn't it?"

"It's a fundraiser for the ER, yes."

Gavin scrubbed his hand over his face. "Is my job safe?"

Virginia wanted to tell him the truth, but she honestly couldn't. She was sworn to a confidentiality agreement.

"The ER isn't in danger."

It was a lie, one that made her feel sick to her stomach. Gavin walked over to her desk and sat down in front of her.

"You're sure?"

Virginia looked away. "Gavin, I wish I could tell you otherwise, but I'm bound by a legal agreement to keep it secret." Then she looked back at him, trying to convey everything she couldn't say in a look.

"I see." Gavin nodded. "I understand."

"I would tell you."

"I know you would."

"I'll write you a recommendation letter if you want to leave. I understand why you wouldn't want to stay."

"I don't need a letter." Then he reached across the desk and took her hand in his. "I have faith that you'll keep this hospital from going under. I'm not ready to jump ship."

His hand around hers felt so good. It calmed her and made her wish that it wasn't just their bare hands touching. That it could be more.

Virginia took her hand back. "Where did you hear this rumor?"

"Dr. Rogerson."

"Ah, well, that makes sense. She handed in her resignation this morning." Virginia cleared her throat. "I heard you were on a date with Moira. How was it?"

Gavin grinned and leaned back in the chair. "Fine."

Virginia's cheeks flushed. "Oh, that's great. She's a wonderful surgeon."

"Are you jealous, Virginia?" Gavin asked, his green eyes twinkling mischievously.

"Don't be ridiculous. I just wanted to know where the rumor started so I could quash it before it got out of hand. I don't care who you see or don't see, Dr. Brice. You've made it clear that your personal life is no concern of mine and it isn't."

Gavin's smile disappeared and he frowned. "Well, glad that's settled."

Virginia nodded and turned back to her paperwork, effectively dismissing him. "I'd better get some more of this paperwork done and I'll schedule your duty shifts for the evening starting on your next rotation."

"Great. Thanks. I appreciate it." He stood and she watched him as he walked across the room and opened the door. He turned and glanced back. "Good night, Dr. Potter."

"Good night, Dr. Brice."

# CHAPTER TWELVE

"YOU'RE DOING A fantastic job with the benefit, Dr. Potter."

Virginia plastered on her best smile as she walked through the Excelsior downtown San Francisco. "I'm glad you approve, Mr. Shultz." That was what she said, but what she really thought was, I hope this is worth it, because this benefit is already costing the hospital precious amounts of money.

Money that could be used to keep the emergency department open.

She'd been carrying around that information for a month and it was eating her up inside. This benefit had to go off without any kind of hiccup in order to save the emergency department. There were so many people in the department who depended on their jobs. Especially Gavin.

She let her mind wander to him for a brief moment. She hadn't seen him since they'd spoken that night in her office. Though it wasn't unexpected. He'd transferred to nights and she'd been so busy with the gala that there hadn't been a chance to catch up. There had been a few times when she'd caught a fleeting glimpse of him coming in as she was leaving, but that was about it. Although she'd see him soon because she had an appointment to see Lily in about an hour.

Virginia glanced at her wristwatch. "If you'll excuse me, Mr. Schultz, I do have an appointment with a VIP patient."

"Of course, of course, but before you go I just wanted to

confirm with you that Dr. Gavin Brice will be speaking at the event."

"Dr. Brice?"

"Yes," Mr. Schultz said. "Many of the attendees are quite interested in hearing him speak. He may have started as a bit of a rogue, but he's starting to fit in with our hospital. We'd love to have him talk about his experiences with Border Free Physicians."

"Well, I can certainly ask him, but he's not one of the attendings I asked to speak. He's on nights now and I may not be able to pull him away from his duties."

Mr. Schultz frowned. "Then you need to ask him, Dr. Potter. I would advise you to tell him to speak."

Virginia plastered another smile on her face and excused herself from the hotel ballroom.

*"Tell him to speak."*

Like she could order her surgeons to do anything like that.

Still, she had to try and get Gavin onside for the sake of the benefit.

Would it really save the hospital?

Or was it just a temporary patch on the shredded artery?

When she got to the hospital, she changed into her scrubs. When she came out of her office Janice stopped her typing.

"Lily Johnson is waiting for you in exam room 2221A. Dr. Brice is with her."

"Thank you, Janice. Hold my calls."

"Of course."

When Virginia entered the exam room Gavin was sitting with Lily. As were Rosalie and Rose. Gavin was in his scrubs because he was on duty tonight, and it pleased her that he was making time for the girls.

He always had time for his nieces. She admired him for that. First she checked out the X-rays waiting on the light box for her. "Well, it looks like that ulna is all healed. How about we take care of your arm and get that cast off? What do you say to that?"

Lily smiled. "I'm really looking forward to getting it off."

"I bet you are." Virginia readied her tools and smiled at Rose. "How are you today, Rose?"

Rose shrugged but didn't smile.

"Nervous about your sister?" Virginia asked.

Rose nodded.

"There's no reason to be nervous." Virginia picked up the saw used to remove the cast and started it. Rose's eyes widened, her little face paling. "This saw won't cut her skin. You want to know how I know?"

Rose didn't nod but watched the saw in fascination. Virginia placed it against her palm, running the saw over her hand.

"See, it just tickles."

"Cool," Lily said. "That's so cool."

Virginia winked at Gavin, who was hiding his laugh behind his hand. "Okay, Lily, let's get this tired-looking cast off." She slipped goggles and a face mask on the little girl.

"What're these for?"

"It'll protect you from the dust. I have my own pair too."

Lily held her arm still. Virginia slipped on her mask and goggles and set the oscillating saw down through the fiberglass, cutting away at the fibers.

Lily watched, her eyes wide from behind the goggles, until the cast fell away from her pale arm.

"Yuck, it's all weird-looking and it stinks." Lily pinched her nose.

Virginia set down the saw and palpated Lily's arm and then moved it around, asking her if she felt any pain. "Well, your arm's been covered for a month. It hasn't seen the sun in four weeks. Your bone appears to be nice and healed, so I'm begging you, as your doctor, not to hang from any monkey bars at school. Promise me."

Lily grinned. "I promise. Can I keep my cast? I like all the signatures."

"Of course." She turned to Gavin. "Her skin is really dry.

Bathe it in warm water for twenty minutes twice a day and dry it by rubbing gently."

"I know how to take care of a limb after a cast comes off."

Virginia chuckled. "Of course."

"Rosalie, can you take the girls home now?" Gavin asked.

"Of course, Dr. Brice. Come on, girls, you'll see your uncle tomorrow morning."

Virginia helped Lily down and handed her the cast. "Take care of that arm, Lily."

"I will, thank you, Dr. Potter." Lily took Rose's hand and they walked out together.

Virginia watched the girls leave with Gavin's housekeeper. "Dr. Brice, before you start your shift, there's something I need to talk to you about."

Gavin crossed his arms over his chest. "Of course, shoot."

"The board has asked if you would speak at the gala benefit next week."

"No."

Virginia scrubbed her hand over her face. She had half expected that answer from him. "Please, would you do it for the hospital? You offered to help me before with the planning."

"Yes, but that was organizing it. I don't do well with crowds. I don't like giving speeches and I'm sorry but I'm not going to give one for this hospital." He turned to walk away but Virginia stepped in front of him, blocking him from leaving.

"I don't think you quite understand what I'm asking you."

"I do understand what you're asking me, Dr. Potter. The board wants me to talk about all the great adventures I had with Border Free Physicians, but the thing is they *really* don't want me to."

Virginia was confused. "What're you talking about?"

Gavin let out a heavy sigh. "It's not that I don't like speaking to crowds, not really. It's just that I would write a speech, telling all those tuxedoed people exactly what I experienced, the nitty-gritty details of developing countries and how they should be pouring their extra money into helping those less fortunate. Even here, in this city, there are countless missions. There are people living in this city, not necessarily on the streets, who need medical attention. They just can't afford it."

Virginia was stunned. "And you're saying that the board wouldn't want you to talk about it?"

He nodded. "Precisely. I've written my speech countless times in my head. Each time it's edited. I'm not allowed to actually talk about what's needed. The people who buy these expensive plates and bid on the silent auction don't care about what's happening under their noses, let alone in the wider world."

"I will let you speak about that," Virginia said.

Gavin gave her a half-hearted smile. "You say that now, but your hands are tied, Virginia. Don't make a promise that you aren't able to keep."

"I don't think you understand what's really at stake."

"Tell me, then. Tell me what's at stake."

Gavin waited with bated breath for her answer. Though he knew. He'd heard enough rumblings in the hallways about Bayview Grace bleeding out money like its carotid artery had been severed, that the emergency department would most likely be amputated, meaning that he would be out of a job. Moira had been right.

He wanted Virginia to tell him that. Though he knew she couldn't, he still wanted to hear it from her lips all the same.

The staff in the emergency department were stressed, worried about their futures, about their security, and when the staff were stressed, mistakes were made.

Gavin hated working in an environment like that.

What he wanted from Virginia, from his chief of surgery, was for her tell him that this benefit was a last-ditch effort to save the emergency department.

He wanted the truth.

So he waited, watching as Virginia thought of some kind of excuse or story to throw him off the scent.

He'd dealt with stuff like this in Border Free Physicians. He knew how to get around it and he wasn't going to back down until he had the truth.

"You need to speak at the benefit," she said, and straightened her shoulders, crossing her arms in that stubborn stance he knew all too well.

She was going to hold her ground, just as much as he was, and he admired her for that.

"I don't have to speak, Virginia. I'll attend the benefit, but I'm not speaking."

"Yes, you are."

He cocked his head. "I don't think you can force me."

"No, I can't and I really don't want to, but the board has made it clear that you will speak. Just like the other attendings who've been asked. You will speak at the benefit, Dr. Brice."

"Because my job depends on it?"

Virginia didn't utter a word but she nodded, just barely.

*Damn.*

"How bad is it?"

Virginia glanced over her shoulder and then shut the door to the exam room. "It's bad."

"So the emergency department really is on the chopping block?"

"You know I'm betraying a confidentiality agreement. I could get sued."

"I won't breathe a word." And he wouldn't.

She sighed and her face paled.

"How bad is it? Is it just the ER?" he asked.

"A few departments, actually."

Gavin leaned against the wall. The last thing he wanted to do was uproot the girls, but the other hospitals weren't hiring attendings, and there was no way he was going to take up Moira's offer to put in a good word at her new workplace. Anyway, he'd burned his bridges with her after she'd walked out on their date.

"I'll give a speech."

Virginia relaxed. "Thank you. It means a lot to me."

"I'm doing it for the hospital, for all the people who depend on their jobs, but can you do one thing for me?"

"It depends," she said skeptically.

"Promise me you'll do it."

"I can't blindly promise, Gavin."

"Oh, but you expected me to blindly promise to speak at an event I don't agree with?" he snapped.

"You're an attending. It's your duty."

He snorted. "It's not my duty to watch the board try and make a bit of money by throwing away what little they have to try and save this hospital, by hosting some snooty benefit."

"Gavin, I really don't want to argue with you."

"Look, I just want you to tell my staff what's on the line. They know something is up and not knowing is stressing everyone out."

Virginia shook her head. "I can't tell, Gavin. They can't know. I can't afford to have some of my staff leave. Not just yet. You promised."

"That's unfair to them. To those who've given Bayview Grace their loyalty."

"My hands are tied."

"No. They're not."

"Don't you think letting them know that their jobs are on the line would be more detrimental to them?" Virginia's face turned crimson, her voice rising. Gavin had never seen her like this before but, frankly, at this moment he didn't care.

He was damn mad.

His staff deserved to know.

"Tell them."

"No, and you'd better keep your word to me that you won't either." She turned on her heel and stormed out of the exam room.

Gavin let her go and let out a string of profanities. He didn't want to fight with her. She was his equal and she rubbed him the wrong way, because she was just as pigheaded as he was.

*Put yourself in her shoes.*

Only at this moment he couldn't do that rationally. He didn't envy her her job or her position one bit, but the way he was feeling now, if he was chief of surgery he'd be warning his employees that this hospital was in danger.

He took a deep calming breath and then saw her logic.

If she did tell the staff, they'd all leave or not care any more about doing a good job, because what was the point if the hospital was doomed?

He was a jackass.

"Hey, I saw you were having some words with the ice queen," Dr. Jefferson said as he wandered into the exam room. "She was on a rampage, from what I saw. What did you say to her?"

"She's not an ice queen. Show some damn respect, Jefferson."

Jefferson frowned. "What has gotten into you?"

"Nothing."

"You're absolutely stressed."

*You think?* Only he didn't respond to him, he just paced back and forth, trying to calm his nerves. "Is there something in particular you wanted, Dr. Jefferson?"

"Yeah, there's been a major crash on Van Ness. A streetcar and a bus. All hospitals are being braced for trauma. We'll most likely be getting the less serious cases..."

Gavin didn't listen to him further. He pushed past Jefferson, grabbing a rubber gown from the closet and heading out the emergency doors. The moment he stepped outside onto the tarmac he could see a large billow of smoke to the west. Most likely from the accident.

The sound of sirens pierced the air.

He just hoped Virginia's decision to keep his staff in the dark was worth it, and he hoped they remained focused enough not to make any mistakes today.

# CHAPTER THIRTEEN

"So, do you have a date?"

Virginia glanced up at Janice, who'd come into her office with a pile of files. "A what?"

Her lips twitched. "A date. You know, where you take someone out you're attracted to."

"No, I don't have a date."

Janice tsked. "I think the chief of surgery, who planned this event no less, should attend the gala with a hunky and gorgeous man on her arm."

Virginia shook her head. "This chief of surgery has been too busy trying to plan this gala and run a hospital to find a date."

"Well, I guess that's a good enough excuse." Janice dropped the pile of files on her desk with a flourish. "Your patient files to go over and report on. Records says you're behind on your reports."

Virginia groaned. "Can't you do it for me?"

Janice snorted. "Do I look like the doctor?"

"I'm not answering that on the grounds it might incriminate me." She grinned up at Janice, who looked unimpressed.

"However, if I was in your position I would be out wrastling me down some handsome hunk as eye candy for my arm."

"Thanks for the advice, Janice. I'll make a note of it." She rubbed her temples.

"You could use a drink," Janice remarked as she left the office.

*I sure could.*

Virginia checked her watch. It was almost seven in the evening. She'd been at the hospital since four that morning. Almost fifteen hours. It was then she realized how long she'd been bent over her desk, planning a party.

Was this what she'd signed on for?

No.

She'd bought a beautiful dress yesterday. Royal blue, but she hadn't gone out with anyone to get it, because she didn't really have any girlfriends. There had been no one to ooh and ahh over it. No one to tell her that her butt looked too big or what shoes would go with it.

And now she'd be attending the gala alone. No one to appreciate the dress, no one to dance with or make her feel sexy.

She couldn't remember the last time she'd gone on a date.

*What about dinner with Gavin?*

Her cheeks flushed at the memory of his kiss. The way his hands had felt around her. The way his eyes had twinkled in devilment, but that hadn't been a date.

Had it?

Who was she kidding? It had been, but like most dates she had, nothing had come of it. She and Gavin were friends, or quasi-friends. She hadn't had a chance to speak to him since she'd taken off Lily's cast and asked him to do the speech.

She hadn't asked. She'd ordered him to and he'd asked her to be up front with the staff, but she'd refused.

In her flurry of work Virginia had seen Gavin around the hospital and she couldn't help but wonder what had happened on that date with Moira Rogerson. Was he still seeing her? Before Moira had left it had been plain to everyone that Moira had had a thing for Gavin, and who could blame her really? Gavin was a handsome, accomplished and desirable man. Even if he was somewhat brusque.

Moira was a pretty woman and Virginia wondered if Gavin was interested in her.

A thought that irked her.

She had no claim on Gavin. He'd kissed her and she'd pushed him away. She'd made it clear that they could never be.

*I have to get out of here.*

Virginia closed her email and shut down her computer. She grabbed her purse and headed out. Janice had gone home for the evening, which was good because Virginia wasn't sure she could take any more teasing about "wrastling up" a man.

When she got outside she headed for her car and then stopped. There was a bar across the road. She'd never set foot in it but it looked like a respectable enough place.

*What the hell?*

She crossed the road and entered the bar. It was dark inside, even though it was still light outside for a quarter to eight. There were a few people in the bar, a couple playing darts, and she recognized a few people from the hospital, but they didn't acknowledge her and why would they? She was the ice queen of Bayview Grace.

Virginia took a seat at the bar.

"What'll it be?" the pretty blonde bartender asked.

"I honestly don't know."

She cocked an eyebrow. "Well, I've heard some strange things in here, but that's a first."

"Really?" Virginia asked. "I guess that fits as it's my first time in a bar."

"Wow." The young woman grinned. "You're a virgin, then."

Virginia noticed a couple of men down at the end of the bar perked up at the mention of the word "virgin."

"What would you recommend?" Virginia asked, changing the subject.

"How about a glass of wine? I have some nice local wines."

Virginia nodded and felt relieved. "That sounds good."

The bartender nodded. "I'll be right back with a nice red."

Virginia glanced around, not knowing where to look. There was a television over the bar, but it was on a sports channel and she had no interest in that.

"Here's a nice red from Napa." The bartender smiled at

her brightly and set the glass down on a napkin. "I hope you enjoy it."

Virginia handed her some money. "I'm sure I will."

The bartender nodded and headed down to the other end of the bar. Virginia took a sip of her wine and read the labels on the bottles of liquor lining the back shelf.

"Now, I would've pegged you for more of a Shiraz type of girl." Gavin sat down on the barstool next to her.

"Fancy seeing you here."

He chuckled. "I could say the same about you."

Virginia shrugged her shoulders. "Janice suggested I should go out and have a drink. Among other things."

"Other things?" Gavin asked. "Now I'm intrigued."

"Janice likes her opinions, however inappropriate or personal, to be known."

"That's for sure."

"What'll it be, Dr. Brice?" the bartender asked.

"The usual, Tamara. Thanks."

Tamara the bartender nodded and pulled out and filled a glass with beer, setting it down in front of him.

"You come here often?"

Gavin nodded. "Lately. Rosalie is a lot like Janice. She felt I needed some release on my night off. Once a week for the last month I've been coming here. I have a beer and then head home."

"You've been coming here enough to know the bartender's name," Virginia remarked.

"See, that's the interpersonal skills I've been working on."

"Kimber in Trauma says you don't know her name yet."

"Who?"

"She says you call her 'Hello Kitty'."

Gavin laughed. "It's her scrubs. She wears a lot of scrubs that remind me of something Lily or Rose would be wearing. I like her, though, she's a good nurse."

"I like her too."

"Was she offended?" Gavin asked.

"You care?"

"Of course." He took a sip of his beer. "I need my staff on the top of their game. I want to prove to your board that the ER is worth saving."

Virginia's stomach knotted. "You haven't mentioned that to anyone?"

Gavin frowned. "Why would I? It's not my job to tell them their jobs are on the line."

Tension settled between them.

"No, you're right, it's not." Virginia set her wineglass down and stood. "I should really get going."

Gavin grabbed her arm. "Where are you going? You haven't even finished your wine."

"I came here to relax, Gavin. I don't want to talk about the hospital."

"I'm sorry. I didn't want to bring it up either. Don't go."

Virginia sat back down. "How is your speech coming along?"

"No work, remember?"

"Sorry." Virginia took a sip of wine. "It seems like work is all I have time for."

"That shouldn't be your priority, but who am I to talk?"

"How are the girls?" She'd missed them and it surprised her how often she thought about them.

"Good." She noticed tension there, something in the way he pursed his lips and the way his brow wrinkled. "Lily hasn't gotten into any more scrapes."

"I'm glad to hear it."

"Do you have a date yet?"

Virginia tried not to choke on the wine in her mouth. Had he just asked her what she thought he'd asked her?

"Pardon?"

"I asked you if you have a date for the benefit." Gavin watched her face for a reaction and he got the one he was expecting. Her eyes widened and pink crept up her neck to form a delectable little flush.

Virginia cleared her throat and began to fiddle with the stem of her wineglass. "I—I haven't had a chance to ask anyone."

*Good.*

"Neither have I, though I've been asked."

She looked up at him through her thick, dark eyelashes. "Oh, who asked you?"

"Does it matter?" he asked.

There was a flash of something which flitted across her face. Jealousy, perhaps. Gavin certainly hoped so.

"How nice for you."

"I'm not going with them, though."

Their gazes met. "Oh, why not?"

Gavin shrugged. "I'm not interested."

"She's pretty, smart, what's not to like?"

"Who are you talking about?"

"Moira Rogerson."

Gavin cocked an eyebrow. "Moira's left Bayview. I haven't seen her since that night I asked you to switch me to the night shift."

"Why? As I said, she's pretty, intelligent…"

Gavin grinned. "Are you trying to convince me to take Moira to the benefit?"

"Well, when all is said and done, it's someone to dance with."

"I don't dance." Gavin finished off his beer and signaled Tamara for another one.

"What's wrong with dancing?" Virginia asked.

"I don't know how to dance. Do you?"

"I do, in fact." She chuckled. "Don't look so shocked."

"And do you like dancing?" he asked.

"Of course. It's one of the perks of this upcoming benefit. I can't stand stuffy dinners but the dancing after the speeches should be quite enjoyable." Virginia smiled at him, making his blood heat. He loved it when she smiled at him, which wasn't very often.

"Then you should have a date."

Virginia groaned. "Not you too."

"Who's been bugging you to get a date?"

"Janice." Virginia snorted. "Something about being the chief, wrestling and arm candy."

Gavin chuckled. "Wrastling?"

"Her words, not mine." Virginia finished off her wine and set the glass down. "I really should go. I have a long day again tomorrow."

"I'll walk you out." Gavin dropped some money on the bar and walked outside with Virginia. The sun was finally setting in the west. It was brilliant, reflecting off the Golden Gate Bridge. Everything around them was warm and tranquil, but soon fall would be coming, though he'd been told that autumn in San Francisco didn't bring with it that fresh crispness as a lot of other places did.

When he'd first arrived a taxi driver had remarked that sometimes October was hotter than the summer.

He slipped his arm through hers and escorted her across the street, dodging a streetcar as they crossed the slow street.

Virginia pulled out her car keys. "Thanks for the company."

"You should come to the bar more often. It's a frequent haunt of staff members."

"I doubt they'd want the ice queen gracing the darkened doorway of their favorite watering hole, then."

"I wouldn't mind." Gavin cleared his throat. "The ice queen isn't such a harridan anymore."

Virginia blushed again and looked away. "I'll see you later, Gavin. Give my best to the girls." She turned to walk away but he stopped her again. "Is there something else I can help you with?"

"Go with me." His pulse was thundering between his ears.

"Pardon?" she asked, stunned.

"Be my date to the benefit."

"You're serious?"

Gavin nodded. "I am. You need a date, I need one and I

can't think of someone I'd rather go with. I have a condition, though."

Virginia crossed her arms. "There's a condition to being my date? This I have to hear."

"Teach me to dance."

Virginia snorted and then laughed. "You're serious?"

"Well, I don't want to embarrass the chief of surgery by trying to whisk her around the dance floor with two left feet."

Her eyes narrowed. "You have a point, but I have to say I've never been asked out before and had to meet certain conditions."

"It's a date, but not really, you said yourself that you can't date someone you work with."

A strange look crossed her face and she appeared a bit disappointed. Just like he'd felt when she'd climbed into that cab after their dinner, but he wasn't doing this as revenge. Gavin wanted the blinders on Virginia to come off and see that it would be okay for them to date. He wanted to date her.

"You're right," she said, breaking the silence. "Of course."

"So is that a yes?"

"Perhaps." She grinned, a devious smile that made him cringe and wonder what he'd just got himself into. "I have a condition too, though."

"Are you in a position to demand conditions? I mean, I've had an offer."

Virginia punched him hard in the arm. "Hey, I can find a date."

"Okay, what's your condition?" Gavin rubbed his arm.

"I get to pick your tux."

"Tux?"

"It's a black-tie benefit. What were you going to wear?" There was apprehension in her voice.

"A nice suit."

Virginia rolled her eyes. "A tux and it'll be of my choosing. I'm not having you show up in your tuxedo shirt and jeans."

"Fine," Gavin agreed grudgingly. "So, do we have a deal?"

Virginia stuck out her hand. "We do."

Gavin took it, but pulled her close. "Since this is a deal on a sort of romantic notion, shouldn't we seal the deal in some other way?"

She was so close he could smell her perfume. Her body was flush against his, her lips soft, moist and beckoning.

"I think a handshake will do." Her voice was shaky as she took her hand back and stepped away. "Shall we go shopping for a tux after your next shift?"

"I'll check with Rosalie, but I'm sure it'll be fine."

Virginia nodded. "Good. Have a good evening, Gavin. I'll see you on Thursday morning."

Gavin watched her walk across the parking lot and he couldn't help but smile to himself. Sure, he'd manipulated her, but Virginia was a stubborn woman. She was a challenge and it'd been some time since he'd been challenged.

Now, if he could only deal with the other troubling aspect of his life and get the girls' grandparents off his case.

He let out a sigh and headed to his car.

Come hell or high water, he was going to get his life worked out.

One of these days.

# CHAPTER FOURTEEN

"I FEEL RIDICULOUS," Gavin shouted from behind the curtain.

"I don't care." Virginia tried to suppress her laughter. "This is part of the deal." The salesman in the tuxedo rental shop shot her a weird glance from behind her, one he didn't think she'd see but which she saw clearly in the full-length mirror.

"I feel ridiculous."

"Shut up, you're just embarrassing yourself."

Gavin snorted and she laughed silently behind her hand. "I still don't understand what's wrong with my gray suit. It worked for other events I've attended in my career."

"It may have been fine for other events, but my benefit is black tie. It has to go off without a hitch." She paused and her stomach knotted as she tried not to think of the reason why her benefit had to go off without a problem.

The ER's head was on the chopping block.

She got up and wandered toward the curtain. "Are you going to let me see or do I have to come in there?"

"You could come in." And then he laughed from the other side of the curtain, which made Virginia's cheeks flush at the thought of him naked behind a thin curtain.

"I can get you a set of tails," she countered.

"No, thanks. I'm coming out."

Virginia stepped back as the curtain slid to one side. Gavin stepped out and her breath caught in her throat just a bit.

The black tuxedo suited him. Finally, she understood that

expression "fits like a glove," because it was like the tuxedo had been made for him. It made her swoon, her stomach swirling with anticipation. He was a fine specimen.

"Well, how do I look?" Gavin straightened his collar a bit and turned. "Better than the scrubs?"

*Much. Much better,* was what she wanted to say. "You'll do."

He cocked an eyebrow. "Just do?"

"Well, I still think you should wear tails."

Gavin snorted. "No tails."

The salesclerk came over and took some measurements and Virginia watched, trying not to laugh. Gavin looked so unimpressed, but he looked so dashing. Like James Bond, but a more rugged Bond. Instead of the fancy British cars James Bond drove, this version of him drove a motorcycle.

"I'll get this order ready for you and you can change." The salesclerk rolled his eyes as he walked past Virginia.

"What did you do to the poor sales associate?"

Gavin grinned like a devil. "I coughed when he was doing my inner leg."

Virginia couldn't contain her laughter any more. "You're going to drive that poor man to drink."

Gavin shrugged. "I like having fun."

"Could've fooled me, the way you march around that ER."

His easy demeanor faded. "There's no time for frivolity there. If we relax even for a moment, a mistake might happen."

"I respect that kind of drive."

Gavin cocked an eyebrow. "It has nothing to do with drive, it's survival."

"Survival?"

"You've hinted in no uncertain terms that our department is poised to take the axe. We have to run like a well-oiled machine."

Virginia swallowed the lump that formed in her throat. "This benefit will change everything. If we raise enough money and get more investors on board, the ER won't close."

"Virginia, don't lie to me. The signs are on the wall. Mr.

Schultz wants a private clinic to cater to the rich. He's just looking for an excuse to let the hammer fall."

She wanted to tell him he was wrong, but she couldn't because she'd thought the same thing more than once.

"Well, the tuxedo suits you. No pun intended." She hugged herself and walked away as he retreated back to the change room.

She wandered to the front window of the shop and watched the streetcars go by on Market Street. The light outside was getting dim and a fog bank was rolling in, but the fog bank was still high and wouldn't affect them as they were at the foot of San Francisco's many hills.

Gavin came out and paid his deposit and they walked outside together. The air was a bit nippy, but Virginia didn't mind this weather.

South Dakota, at this time of year, was a heck of a lot colder. She hadn't been back home in years. It was late September now and hunting season would be starting. De Smet was a sleepy town for the most part, except for the summer, when the Laura Ingalls Wilder pageants took over the town, and the fall, during hunting.

In a couple of months the temperature would drop and the snow would begin to fly and, boy, would it ever. The open vastness of the Dakota prairies would cause whiteout conditions that rivaled those of Alaska and Canada.

San Francisco didn't get snow like that and for the first time in a long time she was missing it. They walked along Market and then headed uphill towards Union Square. The place where they'd met on their first date.

After that she'd sworn to herself she'd never let that happen again, yet here she was, walking with him back to that same place.

*What am I doing?*

"What're you thinking about?"

"Home," Virginia said.

"Where are you from again?"

"De Smet, South Dakota."

"Not far from Billings, where I grew up." He winked. "Although I've lived in many other places. My parents' jobs always forced Casey and I to be uprooted. I hated constantly moving around."

"Yet you worked with Border Free Physicians?"

"I liked what they represent and I didn't have a family I was uprooting. I would never move the girls. San Francisco is where I'll stay."

"Most army brats aren't so bitter about being moved around."

Gavin sighed. "My parents weren't very… They loved us, but their military careers were their priority and they weren't overly affectionate. Casey and I had no other family. I took care of my sister a lot."

"How did they die?"

"My father was killed in the line of duty the year I went away to college. My mother—my mother committed suicide a year later. She had undiagnosed post-traumatic stress from Iraq. My father's death caused her to snap. Casey was fresh out of high school and married the girls' father the year that happened."

"I'm sorry."

Gavin nodded. "Thanks. It was hard."

"I can understand your devotion to your nieces and wanting to give them that stability. I can see why Casey chose you over the girls' grandparents."

"Yes." Gavin's brow furrowed and she wondered if she'd touched a sore spot. "What about your family? Why haven't you gone home in a long time?"

Virginia hesitated. She never talked about her family to anyone. She didn't want people to know about where she came from. She'd made that mistake before and once people knew they judged her, and she didn't want that.

And she didn't go home because of Shyanne. Everything

reminded her of Shyanne and it hurt too much, even after all this time.

The day Shyanne had died, a piece of her had died too.

"My parents live in a trailer, remember? There wouldn't be room for me to visit." Only her voice cracked with emotion she couldn't hold in.

"What's wrong?"

"It's too painful for me to go back."

They stopped in the square and she was glad for the bit of fog that rolled in as she blinked away the tears that were threatening to spill.

"What happened?" Gavin asked.

Virginia shook her head, but he wouldn't take no for an answer and he ushered her into a small café. The maître d' sat them in the back and Gavin ordered two coffees.

"What happened?" he asked again. "I've spilled some of my secrets so it's time for you to pay up."

She smiled, but barely. Her lips quivered slightly. "I'm a twin."

"Really?"

"Shyanne was my best friend, she was…" Virginia couldn't continue.

"How did she die?" Gavin asked, his voice gentle. His eyes kind.

"Ectopic pregnancy. Something so easy to take care of and diagnose, but I come from a very poor family. Shyanne got pregnant in the last year of high school. The guy took off and she didn't tell anyone because Dad couldn't afford health care insurance. He could barely afford to keep food on the table for the seven of us. Her tube ruptured and by the time they opened her up to do a salpingo-oophorectomy she was gone."

"I'm sorry. I'm surprised you didn't take up a job like I had, to help the underprivileged."

"Are you judging me now?" she snapped.

"No, I'm just curious."

"Who do you think pays for their health insurance now?"

Virginia played with an empty packet of sweetener lying on the table. "Besides, my dad told me to get a job and work hard and keep it."

Gavin nodded. "I understand you a bit better."

Virginia snorted. "Should I be worried?"

"No, but I'm surprised your dad still doesn't have a job."

Virginia sighed. "He's disabled. He was a welder but was hurt on the job. He gets disability checks."

"So how many siblings do you have?"

"Two sisters left and two brothers. The sisters have moved out, but my two brothers are still in high school."

"Must've been nice, having a big family like that."

Virginia smiled. "It was. It is."

"Do you miss them?" he asked.

"I do, but I haven't been back since Shyanne died. Let me rephrase that. I tried once or twice, but it was too hard."

"Don't you get lonely around the holidays?"

"I could ask the same about you, Gavin."

Gavin gave her a half-smile. "It's hard to miss family when you're working."

"Exactly."

And that made Virginia a little sad. Kids and family had never been part of her plan, just working hard and making sure that she had a decent roof over her head and that none of her other siblings would have to die the way Shyanne had. That was what drove her.

She worked holidays and she didn't mind.

Holidays hadn't been extravagant when she was a child and she blocked most of her childhood memories, but one hit her.

Shyanne and her creeping out to the living room in the trailer to see if Santa had come, and that year he had. Their little stockings had had a bulge in the toe.

They'd curled up together on the couch, huddled together while a blizzard raged outside, and just watched the glow of the Christmas lights dancing off the old orange shag rug in the living room, waiting until everyone woke up in the morning and they could see what Santa had brought them.

Santa had brought her a toy pony, with pink hair.

She still had it in her apartment, packed away.

Last Christmas she'd run the ER and racked up a considerable amount of time in the OR. She'd been so happy.

Until she'd got the messages on her phone when she'd got home after a long shift at the hospital. Her mother begging her to come home, her mother wishing her a merry Christmas and telling her how much she missed her.

"Sorry for depressing you," Gavin said, breaking the silence as they finished their coffees. "Must be the fog."

"Must be."

"So, you said you were going to teach me how to dance?"

Virginia smiled. "I'm off tomorrow. I can stop by your place."

"The girls would be happy to see you."

"And I them."

Gavin grinned. "Good, it's a date, then."

"You weren't kidding. You seriously suck at dancing." Virginia winced as Gavin stepped on her toe again. Good thing they weren't wearing shoes. Even with the heels she had picked out for her dress, Gavin would still tower over her, which made her feel dainty. She was five ten and hardly ever met a man who towered over her.

"I'm good at head-banging if you put on some heavy metal." He moved away from her and selected a rock song from his music player, one that you couldn't dance to. At least, that's what she thought.

Virginia crossed her arms. "How am I supposed to teach you to dance to that?"

Gavin grinned and took a step towards her. "Maybe we should practice with a slow song?"

A lump formed in her throat, her mouth going dry, and he was just inches from her. She was suddenly very nervous about his arms around her, about being so close to him. They'd kissed, that memory was burned into her brain, but they were alone in the house, not out on the Embarcadero in public view.

His hands slipped around her waist, resting at the small of her back with a gentle touch, and he took her right hand in his left.

"I think this is correct?"

"Well, in proper ballroom dancing your right hand should be just below my shoulder blade."

"I like it where it is."

"You want to learn this properly, don't you?"

"My apologies, Ginger."

Virginia rolled her eyes and he slid his hand up her back. "Thank you."

"Where did you learn the proper stance for ballroom dancing?"

Virginia winked. "Google."

Gavin laughed and she began to lead him in a slow dance, but soon she wasn't leading and it was Gavin waltzing them around the room.

"I thought you said you didn't know how to dance?" she accused him.

"I have hidden depths, Dr. Potter." He grinned. "I don't know how to fast-dance, but I do know some of the basic slow-dance moves."

"And where did you learn these basic moves?"

"Junior high."

"Junior high, huh? So who was the girl?"

"You know me so well." Gavin winked. "Her name was Kirsten and I wanted to take her to the semi-formal and impress her with my mad skills. So I signed up for dance class, which was taught after school by the aging and venerable Ms. Ward, who smelled keenly like beef vegetable soup and heat rub."

Virginia laughed out loud. "And did Kirsten appreciate your efforts?"

Gavin sighed. "No, she decided to go to the semi-formal with Billy Sinclair."

"The hussy!"

Gavin laughed and then dipped her, bringing her back up slowly until their faces were just inches apart. Virginia's pulse thundered in her ears, being so close to his lips, so close but so far away.

"You're a fine dancer, Dr. Potter. A better teacher than Ms. Ward was, and you smell better too."

"I hope I don't smell like soup." She grinned and gazed up into his eyes, and her heart stuttered just briefly, being pressed so tight against him.

This was a dangerous position to be in.

"You smell a million times better." He touched her face, brushing his knuckles against her cheek and causing a shudder of anticipation to course through her.

Virginia braced herself for a kiss, one she wanted, one that she hadn't stopped thinking about for a long time, but he moved away when the front door opened. This was soon followed by loud shrieking and what sounded like a herd of wild elephants storming up the stairs.

They broke apart as Lily and Rose burst into the living room.

"Dr. Potter," Lily said with enthusiasm that matched the bright smile on her face.

Rose just waved but still didn't say anything.

Rosalie came up next. "Sorry, Dr. Brice. I didn't know you had company."

"No, it's okay, Rosalie. I should be going."

"Aww." Lily pouted. "Can't you stay for dinner tonight, Dr. Potter?"

Virginia glanced at Gavin and he shrugged his shoulders. "It's just hot dogs and hamburgers on the barbecue."

"Please stay, Dr. Potter," Lily begged.

"All right," Virginia said, capitulating. It had been some time since she'd had a real home-cooked barbecue.

Lily shouted her pleasure and Rose jumped up and down excitedly.

"Come, girls, let's get washed up for dinner." Rosalie ushered Lily and Rose from the room.

"Is there something I can help with?" Virginia asked.

"There's a plate of hamburgers and a package of hotdogs in the fridge. If you grab them, I'll get the grill heated up."

"Sure." Virginia made her way to the back of the house where the kitchen was. She opened the fridge and pulled out the hamburgers and hotdogs. As she bumped the fridge door shut with her hip a piece of paper fluttered down to the floor.

She cursed under her breath and set down the meat on the kitchen table so she could pick up the piece of paper.

Virginia glanced at it and did a double take when she saw it was a petition for custody. The girls' paternal grandparents, who were stationed in Japan, were suing Gavin for full custody of the girls. Or had. Virginia's stomach sank when she saw the judgment was attached and was momentarily relieved when she saw they'd been denied, but only on the grounds that Gavin had a good steady job in the girls' hometown and uprooting them would be cruel.

If that changed, according to the judgment, Gavin would lose custody of Lily and Rose. Virginia folded the paper up again, feeling guilty for prying. If Gavin had wanted to tell her this, he would've.

She placed it back on the top of the fridge and sank down in a nearby chair. His job was what kept the girls in his custody. If he lost it and had to uproot the girls, their grandparents would get them.

And his job depended on her, the benefit and her ability to keep Bayview Grace from turning into a private clinic. She couldn't bear it if she was responsible for Gavin losing the girls.

"Hey, the barbecue is ready," Gavin called through the open kitchen window. "Bring me those dogs, chief."

"I'll be right there." Virginia took a deep, calming breath and headed outside.

Lily and Rose were kicking a ball back and forth while Rosalie sat in a lawn chair with a glass of iced tea.

She handed Gavin the plate.

"Are you okay, Virginia?" he asked.

"What? Yes, I'm fine."

"You seem like you're in a bit of a daze."

"I'm okay. Really." She wandered over to the table and poured herself a glass of iced tea. The sun was setting, making the whole scene in the backyard glow with warmth. Virginia smiled. Everyone was so happy and she couldn't understand why the girls' grandparents would want to destroy this.

She would do everything in her power to convince the board not to close the ER. *It wouldn't be my fault.*

Only it would. She was Chief of Surgery.

There was no way she was going to be responsible for tearing apart this family. A family she desperately wished she was a part of.

# CHAPTER FIFTEEN

VIRGINIA WAS STARING off into space again when her inbox pinged with a new email. She wasn't going to bother with it, except she saw it was from Boston General. An old colleague from her intern years was working there.

Out of curiosity she opened it and her breath caught in her throat when she realized it was a job offer.

It was for the head of their level-one trauma center. It wasn't Chief of Surgery, but the salary was good and there would be an extensive amount of research money at her disposal. Her friend had recommended her for the job. Boston General wanted her. They were impressed by how she'd managed to salvage Bayview Grace and it was a tempting, tempting offer.

And then guilt assuaged her. Her career path was secure, but Gavin's and those of the rest of the ER staff were not.

"You're still here?" Janice asked, barging into Virginia's office.

"Of course. Why wouldn't I be?"

Janice raised her eyebrows. "Have you seen the time?"

Virginia glanced at her phone and realized it was a quarter to three. "Darn." She was running late for her hair appointment. The benefit was tonight, the very benefit that was going to make or break this hospital.

"Thanks for the reminder, Janice." Virginia grabbed her purse.

"So, you still haven't told me what piece of hot man flesh you managed to wrangle up to take you to the benefit."

Virginia rolled her eyes. "Sometimes I think you take too many hormones."

Janice snorted. "Cheap shot, Ice Queen. Now, come on and spill the beans."

Virginia tried to suppress her smile. "Dr. Brice is accompanying me to the benefit."

"As in Dr. Gavin Brice?" Janice's mouth dropped open like a fish gasping for air. "You're joking, right?"

"No, I'm not. Dr. Brice is my date for tonight. Why is that so hard to believe?"

"I guess because of how many times he's been hauled into the principal's office." Then she grinned. "Perhaps that's *why* he has been."

Virginia shook her head. "I'm going to be late."

"Please, tell me you're wearing something drop-dead sexy."

"What is up with you?" Virginia asked as she put on her coat.

"Just living vicariously. Now, tell me about the dress."

"You're the one who told me I was going to be late."

"I guess I'll have to wait to see it tonight." Then she grinned, one of those grins like the Cheshire cat in *Alice in Wonderland* would give.

Virginia shook her head. "I'm going to send you for a tox screen. I swear sometimes you're dipping into the sauce."

Janice laughed. "Hey, as I said, just living vicariously. I'm glad for you."

"Glad?"

"I like you and I want to see you happy." Janice shrugged. "Now, go on, get out of here and get all made up. Knock his socks off."

Virginia smiled and left. Janice may be all up in her business at the best of times, but the woman really was the closest thing she'd had to a friend since she'd become Chief of Sur-

gery and the closest thing to an overbearing and overprotec-
tive mother since she'd moved out here.

The next shift of physicians was arriving. Physicians who
were going to work the night shift while a lot of the department heads were at the benefit.

Virginia avoided making eye contact with anyone. She was
tired of being stopped and asked questions about the future of
Bayview Grace and whether this benefit would help.

As far as she was concerned, she didn't believe it would.
She felt like she was delaying the inevitable, but the board
was very keen on the idea and she knew it was for them. The
rich investors who liked to have a good party. Having this
benefit and raising money would make them feel good later
when they dropped the axe on the trauma department of the
hospital.

*"Que bueno,* Dr. Brice!"

"Yeah, you look handsome," Lily gushed. "And I bet she
won't recognize you since you shaved off your scruffies."

Rosalie laughed and Rose grinned.

"Why are you laughing, Rosalie? Uncle Gavin's scruffies
were weird and patchy. He looks good with a shaved face."

Gavin sighed and straightened the black bow tie. He felt
like an overstuffed penguin in this tux, but when he'd tried it
on, Virginia's face had flushed and he'd known she approved.

"I'm uncomfortable," he muttered.

"Of course you are, Dr. Brice, but just think how your
*querida* will light up when she sees you."

"Dr. Potter is *not* my *querida.*" Though he wanted her to be.

Rosalie cocked an eyebrow in disbelief. "Sure. Lily, don't
you have a present for your uncle?"

"Right!" Lily leapt down from the bed and ran out of the
room. Gavin heard the fridge door open and Lily came running back with two clear boxes and handed him one. "It's your
boutonniere."

"My what?"

Rosalie stepped forward and took the box from him, opening it and then pinning the spray on his lapel. "I did this for my son when he was going to prom."

"I'm not going to prom," Gavin said. "It's a benefit."

Rosalie tsked under her breath. "Let them have their fun. They were so excited to buy you one."

Gavin felt a bit goofy with the small white carnation and spray of baby's breath pinned to his lapel, but overall he felt uncomfortable. He was used to jeans and a T-shirt, not this penguin suit. He glanced at Rose, who was sitting cross-legged on the floor in front of the full-length mirror.

"How do I look, Rose?"

Rose grinned and gave him a thumbs-up, before scrambling to her feet and leaving the room.

"I'll take that as a compliment," Gavin murmured. "What's the other box for?"

"It's for Dr. Potter," Lily said, holding it out. "It's a wristlet."

Gavin ruffled Lily's head. "Thanks, I'll tell her it's from you."

"No, you can't do that, Uncle Gavin. You have to tell her it's from you." Lily handed him the box. "You look worried."

"I'm a little worried that you're getting so excited about this. It's a work thing really."

"Don't worry, Dr. Brice. The girls just aren't used to you getting all dressed up and going out." Rosalie straightened his tie. "You look good. Go and have some fun. Don't come home until after your shift tomorrow."

"Fun is not something I'm planning on having."

Rosalie shook her head. "Dr. Potter is a very attractive woman."

Gavin cleared his throat and patted his jacket. "Shoot, have you seen some cue cards? My speech is written on there."

"On your dresser," Rosalie said. "Now, come, Lily, let's leave your uncle in peace to finish up and we'll watch for the limo."

"Limo?" Gavin asked. "I didn't order a limo."

Rosalie grinned deviously. "I know, Dr. Brice. You were going to pick up the chief of surgery in the minivan. I think not."

"Rosalie, you're going to be the death of me."

Rosalie just laughed and shut the door to the bedroom. Gavin let out a nervous breath he hadn't realized he'd been holding and smoothed down his hair again. His usual cowlick of hair wasn't standing on end. It was actually tame tonight. It was weird that he'd shaven off his "scruffies," as Lily so eloquently put it, but he wanted to make a good impression.

And not on the board.

Everything he was doing was for Virginia.

"The limo is here, Uncle Gavin!" Lily shouted down the hall.

"Thanks." Gavin picked up the wristlet Lily had picked out for Virginia. It was a bright bubblegum hue of pink.

*Always pink.*

The limo had better not be pink.

He said his quick goodbyes to the girls and headed outside, breathing a sigh of relief when he saw the limo was black. It was sleek and sophisticated. Even though he planned to give Rosalie a stern talking to for hiring a limo, he decided that it had been a smart thing to do.

He gave the driver Virginia's address and climbed into the back.

It was a short drive to Virginia's Nob Hill apartment and he realized he'd never been to her place before.

Her apartment was in a modern-looking building halfway up the steep hill. He pushed her buzzer.

"Who is it?"

"It's me. Gavin."

"Come on up."

The door unlocked and Gavin entered the lobby. Her apartment was on the third floor, so he didn't bother waiting for the elevator. Instead he took the stairs, trying to calm his nerves.

Virginia's apartment was at the end of the hall. He took a deep breath and knocked.

Virginia opened the door and his breath was taken away at the sight of her. He'd known she was going to be dressed up, but he hadn't mentally prepared himself for what he was seeing. Her hair was swept up off her shoulders in a French twist at the back, but it wasn't the hairstyle that caught his attention. It was the creamy long neck that was exposed to him, thanks to the dress she was wearing.

The color was a deep royal blue, which set off her coloring perfectly. It was a one-shoulder dress, but it had lace across the shoulder and the bodice. There was beige fabric underneath to hide any nudity, but you couldn't tell there was fabric there. The intricate lace flowers looked like they were painted on her skin.

There were a few sequins that made the dress sparkle in the light. The dress hugged her curves, clinging to her in all the right places, and there was a slit up the left side, almost to her thigh.

Her legs were long, lean and he had a mental image for a brief moment of them wrapped around his waist.

His breath was literally taken away and he knew he wouldn't be able to mumble any two words together coherently.

What he wanted to do was scoop her up and take her to the bedroom to show her just how much he liked her dress.

"How do I look?" she asked, and did a spin.

"Wow." It was all he managed to get out.

Virginia cocked an eyebrow. "Wow? That's it?"

"I—I don't know what else to say." *I could show you exactly what I think about you wearing that dress.* "You look stunning."

She blushed. "Thank you."

"The color is becoming."

Virginia gave him a strange look and then shut and locked her door. "So, should we take my car?"

"No, I have that taken care of."

Gavin held out his arm and she took it as they walked to the elevator.

"Well, I guess no one will see us arrive in the minivan."

Gavin snorted. "It's not the minivan."

"The motorcycle?" She frowned. "I don't want to ruin my hair."

He shook his head. "You'll see."

As they walked into the elevator she cocked her head to one side and then touched his face gently. "You shaved! I don't think I've ever seen you without…"

"Scruffies, as Lily calls them. Yes, she was quite impressed I'd shaved my scruffies off."

Virginia chuckled. "You do clean up nice, Gavin."

"As do you."

They rode the elevator down to the lobby and she gasped in surprise when she saw the limo. "Oh, Gavin. Wow."

"Now who's using wow?" he teased, and opened the door for her. As she climbed inside, Gavin caught another glimpse of her creamy-white leg and took another deep breath. He slid in beside her and shut the door.

"Can you take us to the Excelsior on Market, please?" Gavin asked.

"I will, sir, but I was told to take you on a small little drive first. There's some complimentary champagne in the bucket. We'll arrive at the Excelsior at six-thirty." The driver put up the privacy screen.

Gavin looked at Virginia apologetically. "Are we going to be late?"

She shook her head. "No, the happy hour is from six to seven and it's only five-thirty. Let's enjoy ourselves."

"Okay. Oh, but first I have something for you." He reached for the clear box. "I'm sorry, it's bright pink."

Virginia giggled. "The girls?"

"I'm not supposed to say. You don't have to wear it."

"No, I love it. Pink goes with blue." She held out her hand. "Besides, I didn't get to go to prom. This is fun."

Gavin opened the box and then slid the wristlet onto her, but before he let go of her hand he brought it up and pressed his lips against her knuckles.

"Gavin," she whispered. "You know…"

"I know." He knew her feelings on dating, but he couldn't help himself. He was falling in love with Virginia, in spite of everything. He'd never thought he'd feel this way about a woman, but he was falling head over heels for her.

"How about we have some of that champagne? It might take the edge off for your upcoming speech."

"Good idea." Gavin found the champagne and handed Virginia a flute. He popped the cork and poured them both a glass. "To a successful benefit tonight."

"Cheers."

He hated champagne, preferring beer, but he downed it as quickly as he could. He wanted the alcohol to numb him from the nervousness he felt about his upcoming speech, about the security of his job at Bayview Grace, and to keep him from pressing Virginia down against the leather seat and taking her, like he desperately wanted to.

Tonight was going to be a long night.

The limo driver took them up the long figure-eight length of Twin Peaks Boulevard. Gavin didn't really enjoy the twisting and turning. They were gripping the seat of the limo tightly, jostling back and forth from the drive up the Eureka North Peak.

"Whose idea was this?" Virginia asked.

"Most likely Lily's. She said Casey used to speed up this hill and it was like being on a roller coaster."

Virginia chuckled. "I can see why."

One sharp turn caused her to slide across the seat and fall against his chest, her hand landing right between his legs.

"Gavin, I'm so sorry." She moved. "I wasn't expecting such a sharp turn."

"Don't apologize. I understand." What he wanted to tell her was he didn't mind in the slightest. It was nice having her so close, even if her hand had landed dangerously close to possibly injuring him.

The limo driver took them to Christmas Tree Point, which had the best vantage point over the entire city and the bay. The driver got out and opened the doors. Gavin grabbed the champagne glasses as Virginia wandered over to the railing. The wind, surprisingly, was not strong and there was no fog rolling from the Pacific to obstruct the view.

There was a breeze and it whipped at Virginia's dress, making it swirl and ripple like deep blue waves. A smile was on her face and she sighed as he handed her a full glass of champagne.

"Whatever happens tonight with the benefit, you should be proud. It's quite a feat for a prairie girl."

She grinned and took a sip of her champagne. "Lily's idea was good. You'll have to mention it to her."

Gavin chuckled and moved closer. "I will."

"I love this view." She sighed again. "So different from vast prairie."

"I've been through South Dakota, there are some rolling hills."

"The Wessington Hills. Yes, to the west, but where I come from it's just prairie. Don't get me wrong, I love it but I think I love this more."

Gavin leaned on the railing. "It is quite beautiful. I can see why my sister chose to settle here."

"Have you ever been up here before?" Virginia asked.

"No, this is my first time." He straightened and took her empty glass from her, setting it down on a bench so he could cup her face. "I'm glad I could share it with you."

"Me too," she whispered. Her cheeks were rosy and he wasn't sure if it was the nip in the air, the champagne or whether she was feeling something for him.

Gavin hoped it was the latter.

He tipped her chin so she was forced to look at him. Her

eyes were sparkling in the fading sunlight. The sun was going down behind her, giving her the appearance that she was glowing.

"Gavin..."

"I know what you're going to say."

"You do?"

He nodded. "I do, but I'm going to do it anyway."

Before she could interrupt him again he kissed her, gently. Though it took all his strength to hold back the passion he was feeling for her right now. There was something so right and perfect about this kiss and he hoped it wasn't going to end up as badly as the first one had.

Virginia moved in closer, her hand touching his cheek and then sliding around to the nape of his neck, her fingers tangling in his hair. It made his blood heat.

He wanted her. Right here. Right now.

Virginia broke off the kiss and leaned her forehead against his. "I think—I think it would be wise if we head back downtown."

Gavin nodded and fought the desire coursing through him. "You're probably right."

She grinned, her eyes still twinkling. "I know I'm right. You're a dangerous man, Gavin." Then she blushed again and moved past him towards the limo. The driver, who'd discreetly returned to the driver's seat while they'd been making out, jumped out and opened the door for Virginia.

Gavin watched her climb back into the limo, catching just a glimpse of her bare leg through the slit in her dress.

*What does she mean by saying I'm a dangerous man?*

A grin broke across his face as he thought about the possibilities, but the one that excited him most was that he affected her just as much as she affected him.

He wanted her. More than that, he was almost sure that he was falling in love with her. Maybe he wasn't the only dangerous individual here tonight.

Virginia was just as dangerous as he was.

# CHAPTER SIXTEEN

VIRGINIA COULDN'T TAKE her eyes off Gavin. When she walked in on his arm, she saw the looks of envy and admiration from the other women in the room. Gavin cleaned up nicely. She liked him all rough and rugged, but she liked him this way too, in a tuxedo, looking svelte.

When Virginia caught Janice's eye from across the room, Janice winked and gave her a thumbs-up, which made Virginia blush, but Janice was right. Gavin was a fine specimen and it was taking all her strength not to jump into his arms like some kind of teenage girl.

And that kiss up on Christmas Tree Point was burned into her lips. And into her mind. And it was all she could do to keep her wits about her. All she wanted to do was drag Gavin out of the room and have her way with him.

Which shocked her.

*Get a hold of yourself.*

Instead, she made sure they were mingling, that they weren't alone together, and she was pleasantly surprised at how charming and affable he was to the board members and investors. Even Mrs. Greenly, who'd nearly been trampled by Gavin on a gurney just a couple of months ago, was conversing with him and then checking him out when he wasn't looking.

Though she couldn't blame Mrs. Greenly one bit.

Gavin looked so fine.

He was up on the stage now, talking to the board about his

work and how important trauma medicine was to Bayview Grace, but Virginia couldn't make out a word. All she heard were muffled sounds like Charlie Brown's teachers would make on the old cartoon specials.

*It has to be the champagne.*

The stuff they'd had in the limo was top-end champagne and she'd had a couple of glasses. Well, more than a couple. She'd had four and she was feeling happy at the moment. Not drunk, just relaxed. She hadn't planned on drinking so much before the benefit, but being trapped in that limo with Gavin as they'd gone on a little scenic drive up the twin peaks had been more than Virginia could handle.

The whole time she'd just wished that the driver would make himself scarce so they could make out in the backseat. Like teenagers.

She'd fallen in love with Gavin. She didn't know when or how, she just realized it now, but she really didn't have any chance with him because every time he'd tried with her, she'd shot him down.

The sensible side of her, the chief of surgery side, had turned him down flat.

As long as they worked at Bayview Grace and she was chief, there was no way they could date.

Unless she took that job, but that new job was across the country and Gavin had already stated he wasn't going to uproot the girls and she didn't blame him one bit.

There was applause and Virginia realized the speech had come to an end. She clapped in enthusiasm and moved up on the stage to give her little spiel and thank the people who had spoken this evening.

Gavin passed her on the stairs and flashed her an encouraging smile, one that made her knees knock together and her blood heat.

She only hoped no one would see her blush up on stage.

"Thank you, Dr. Brice, for your impassioned speech about trauma care at Bayview Grace. I want to thank all my esteemed colleagues for taking time out of your hectic schedules and speaking here tonight about our hospital. I also want to thank the board of directors and their guests. Bayview Grace runs on the generosity of caring individuals such as yourselves. Our hospital has come a long way in the two short years I've been Chief of Surgery and I know with your continued support we can go much further. The dance floor is being cleared and our band is ready. Please, enjoy your evening here and thank you all again." Virginia smiled and acknowledged the applause as she left the stage.

"You're very good at PR, Dr. Potter," Gavin teased as she took a seat beside him.

"It's all part of the job." They were alone at the table, as everyone was getting up to mix and mingle as the band warmed up.

"Do you enjoy it, though, or would you prefer to be in surgery?"

"That's not a fair question, Gavin."

He cocked an eyebrow. "Why not?"

"I like being Chief of Surgery," she stated, and only because no one else was sitting at their table at that moment. "I would like it even more if I had more OR time. Are you happy?"

Gavin grinned. "Very."

"I find that hard to believe."

"Why?" he asked.

"Because you're not off trekking around the world. You made it very clear to me several times you'd rather be anywhere but here."

Gavin hung his head in defeat. "That was before."

"Before what?"

Gavin opened his mouth to say something else but Mr. Schultz approached the table. "Excellent speech, Dr. Brice. I didn't think you had it in you."

Gavin plastered a fake smile across his face. "Neither did I, Mr. Schultz. If you'll excuse me for a moment, I think I'll check on the girls."

Virginia watched Gavin leave the room and wished she could go with him, but Mr. Schultz took his empty seat.

"You did a fine job, Dr. Potter."

"Thank you."

Mr. Schultz sighed. "I hope you'll be able to do the same when we transform Bayview Grace into a private hospital."

Virginia's stomach knotted. "You can't have made the decision already—we haven't even tallied any of the donations and the silent auction isn't even finished."

Mr. Schultz shrugged and downed the glass of Scotch he had in his hand. "The board wants what it wants."

"I think you'll be pleasantly surprised by what we achieve tonight, Mr. Schultz."

He gave her a petulant smile. "We'll see, Dr. Potter. We'll see."

Virginia shot him figurative daggers as he got up and left to schmooze with some rich potential investors.

She was annoyed.

Mr. Schultz didn't care how much money they brought in. In his eyes, the ER was deadweight and he wanted it gone.

A private hospital specializing in plastics and sports medicine would bring in so much more money and all Mr. Schultz saw was the dollar signs. He didn't care about the poor people on the street who came into the ER every day.

Those without insurance or funds to pay for the medical help they needed. Like Shyanne.

*What am I doing?*

Having a good job and security was one thing, but not living by your principles was another. If the ER closed, she would quit. There was nothing else for it. There was no way she could work at a private hospital, treating only the privileged few. That's not why she'd become a doctor and she couldn't help but wonder when her course in life had left that path.

"Are you all right? You look a little pale." Gavin sat down and then poured her a glass of water from the carafe. "Here, have a drink."

"Thanks. It's a bit hot in here." She took a sip of the water, but the lump in her throat made it hard to swallow.

The band started up by playing an old rock ballad from the eighties. One she'd always liked as a child.

"Come on." Gavin took her hand and pulled her to her feet. "Let's dance. You look tense."

Virginia didn't argue as he pulled her out onto the dance floor. Only he didn't hold her in the proper stance she'd lectured him about only a couple of nights ago. His hand rested in the small of her back and this time she didn't argue. She liked the feeling of his strong hand there, guiding her across the dance floor.

"What's wrong?" he asked.

"I told you, it's the crush of people. I'm not good with large crowds."

"You live in the city," he teased.

"I grew up on the prairies." She laughed. "It's so silly."

Gavin shook his head. "No, it's not."

"And you're used to a mad crush."

"I traveled across India by train, remember? This is nothing compared to that."

Virginia shuddered. "I wouldn't like that."

"I wouldn't let you do that. Not dressed the way you are." He leaned in close, his hot breath fanning her neck. "You look good enough to devour."

Her pulse quickened. "Devour?"

"Yes, it's what I've been fighting all evening."

"The urge to d-devour me?" Her voice caught in her throat. Even though she shouldn't press it further, she wanted to. Badly. "Tell me how."

Gavin moaned and held her tighter, her body flush against his. She could feel every hard contour of his chest through their clothes and she wondered what it would be like to feel nothing between them. What it would be like if they were skin to skin, joined as one? The thought made her knees tremble and her stomach swirl with anticipation.

"I would take out the pins in your hair so I could run my fingers through it." The words were whispered close to her ear, making her skin break out in gooseflesh. "Then I would kiss you. I want to taste your lips again."

Virginia closed her eyes and recalled the way his lips had felt pressed against hers. She wanted him. What did she have to lose?

"Go on," she urged.

"Virginia, I don't think I can. Not in decent company." He pulled her tighter and she felt the evidence of his arousal pressed against her hip.

"Come on." Virginia moved away and pulled him off the dance floor.

"Where are we going?"

"I was offered a gratis suite for booking the function at the hotel." She pulled out the key card the hotel had given her this morning when she'd finalized details. Virginia swiped it in the elevator and then glanced nervously at Gavin.

"Are you sure?" he asked.

Virginia kissed him then, showing him exactly how sure she was. She was tired of being alone and for once she wanted to live a little. Take a chance, and Gavin was worth the risk.

The elevator doors opened, but they didn't break their kiss. She just dragged him in, letting her fingers tangle in the hair at the nape of his neck. His tongue pushed past her lips, twining with hers.

The elevator doors opened with a ding and they broke off their kiss. Virginia was glad no one was waiting on the other side, but even that wouldn't have stopped her from her present course.

"Which way?" Gavin asked, his voice husky and deep, rumbling from his chest.

Virginia took his hand and led him down the hall to the suite. She swiped the keycard and opened the door, but before she could cross the threshold Gavin scooped her up in

his arms, claiming her mouth again. He kicked the door shut
with his heel.

The room was dark, except for the thin beam of city lights
through the blackout curtains. Gavin set her down on the floor,
her knees back against the edge of the bed. It made her feel
nervous, but exhilarated her all the same. It felt like the first
time all over again.

If only it was. Her first time hadn't been all that memorable
and the guy hadn't made her feel the way Gavin was making
her feel right now.

She wanted Gavin.

All of him.

She wanted him to possess her. For once she didn't want to
be the boss and she was giving it all to him.

Gavin reached up and undid her hair from the twist, letting it fall against her shoulders. He ran his fingers through it.

"I've been longing to do this since you opened the door to
your apartment and I saw you in that dress."

He kissed her again, just a light one, then he buried his face
against her neck. His hot breath fanned against her skin, making goose pimples break out. A tingle raced down her spine
and she let out a little sigh.

Air hit her back and she realized he was undoing the zip-
per in the back of her dress. She shivered, from nerves and
anticipation.

His lips captured hers in a kiss, his tongue twining with
hers. Gavin's fingers brushed against her bare back before he
trailed them up to slip the one shoulder off. Her dress pooled
on the floor. All she was wearing now was her bustier, lace
panties and heels.

It was so risqué.

It thrilled her. Virginia's heart was racing.

"God, you're beautiful. More beautiful than I imagined."

Virginia kicked her heels off and sat down on the bed.
"Come here." And she reached out and pulled him down.

"You'll wrinkle my suit."

"I do hope so." She undid his bow tie and tossed it away. Then helped him take off his tuxedo jacket.

"No throwing that." He stood up, laying the jacket neatly on a chair, and began to undress for her. Her body was awash with flames of desire. She leaned back to watch as he peeled away the layers.

His chest was well-defined and bare. Then he toed off his shoes and socks before he undid his trousers, stepping out of them and hanging them over the chair as well. He was wearing tight boxer briefs and Virginia could see the evidence of his arousal.

Gavin approached the bed and Virginia pulled him until she was kneeling in front of him. His eyes sparkled in the dim room. "I wanted you the moment I saw you, Virginia."

"Even with all my nagging?"

Gavin moaned and then stole a kiss, his fingers tangling in her hair, pulling her closer. "Especially with the nagging."

"Me too," she whispered. Reaching for him, she dragged him into another kiss. His hands slipped down her back, the heat of his skin searing her flesh and making her body ache with desire. Gavin made quick work of her bustier.

Knowing that she was so exposed to Gavin sent a zing of desire through her. He cupped her breasts, kneading them. Virginia let out a throaty moan at the feel of his caresses against her sensitized skin.

Even though he was a surgeon, his hands were surprisingly calloused. Probably from all his years in Border Free Physicians.

Virginia ran her hands over his smooth, bare chest, before letting her fingers trail down to the waist of his boxers. He grabbed her wrists and held her there, before roughly pushing her down on the bed, pinning her as he leaned over her. He released her hands and pressed his body against hers, kissing her fervently.

"Virginia, you drive me wild."

She kissed him again, letting his tongue plunder her mouth. Her body was so ready for him.

Each time his fingers skimmed her flesh, her body ignited, and when his thumbs slid under the sides of her panties to tug them down, she went up in flames.

He pressed his lips against her breast, laving her nipple with his hot tongue. She arched her back, wanting more.

"You want me?" he asked huskily.

*Make me burn, Gavin.*

His hand moved down her body, between her legs. He began to stroke her, making her wet with need.

"I want to taste you. Everywhere."

Virginia didn't even have a chance to reply. His lips began to trail down over her body, across her stomach and down to the juncture of her thighs. When he began to kiss her there, she nearly lost it.

Instinctively, she began to grind her hips upward; her fingers slipping into his hair and holding him in place. She didn't want him to stop. Warmth spread through her body like a wildfire across the prairie.

She was so close to the edge, but she didn't want to topple over. She wanted him deep inside her.

"Hold on, darling."

Virginia moaned when he moved away. He pulled a condom out of his trouser pocket and put it on. She was relieved. Being with him had made her so addle-brained she'd completely forgotten it.

"I see you've planned for all contingencies," she teased.

"Honestly, I just remembered it was in there. Thank goodness, it is. It's a force of habit from my wilder days."

"I'm glad that's a habit you haven't broken."

"Damn straight. Now, where were we?"

He pressed Virginia against the pillows and settled between her thighs. Gavin shifted position and the tip of his shaft pressed against her folds. She wanted him to take her, to be his.

Even though she couldn't be.

He thrust quickly, filling her completely. She clutched his shoulders as he held still, stretching her. He was buried so deep inside her.

"I'm sorry, Virginia," he moaned, his eyes closed. "You feel so good." He surged forward and she met every one of his sure thrusts.

"So tight," he murmured again.

Gavin moved harder, faster. A coil of heat unfurled deep within her. Virginia arched her back as pleasure overtook her, her muscles tightening around him as she came. Gavin's thrusts became shallow and soon he joined her in a climax of his own.

He slipped out of her, falling beside her on the bed and collecting her up against him. She laid her hand on his chest, listening to his breathing.

"That was wonderful," she whispered.

"It was."

As Virginia lay beside Gavin in silence, the only sounds the city of San Francisco and his breathing, she couldn't help but wonder what she'd done. She'd made a foolish mistake. She'd slept with a fellow employee. Something on her no-no list, but right here, right now she didn't regret it.

This was where she wanted to be and for the first time in a long time she didn't care what happened to her job, and that thought terrified her.

# CHAPTER SEVENTEEN

INCESSANT BUZZING WOKE him from his slumber. When Gavin opened his eyes a crack, the light from the rising sun filtered in through a gap between the hotel room's curtains, blinding him, and he winced. The buzzing continued and he reached over for his phone. He glanced at the clock. It was only five in the morning. It took him a few moments to focus enough to read the words.

"Large incoming trauma. Please report to hospital stat."

*Damn.*

He sent off a quick text to Rosalie about being called in for a trauma, but Rosalie wouldn't mind. She'd take the girls for the whole weekend, she'd said so last night.

It was as if Rosalie had known what was going to happen. He usually hated it when she was right, because she loved to lord it over him, but in this instance he didn't mind.

Not in the least.

Gavin placed his phone back on the nightstand and let out a groan. He rolled over and looked at Virginia, sleeping with her dark hair fanned out over the thick pillow. She looked so peaceful nestled amongst the feather pillows and the feather top. A tendril of her brown hair curled around her nipple and he groaned inwardly as he ran his knuckles gently over her arm.

He remembered every nuance of her. It would be burned on his brain forever. Virginia had been so responsive in his arms.

So hot.

Being buried inside her had been like heaven. He hadn't realized how much he'd wanted her until he'd been joined with her.

When everything else had been pulled away and it had only been them.

Vulnerable. Naked.

Exposed.

Just thinking about her made his passion ignite again. He was so hard and ready for her. Gavin groaned and moved away.

As much as he wanted to spend the morning in bed with her, he couldn't.

A trauma was coming in. All part and parcel of being head of Trauma and he didn't want to give Mr. Schultz any more reason to close the ER.

He'd do anything to help Virginia and make her job easier.

He leaned over and pressed a light kiss against her forehead. Virginia stirred and opened her eyes, but just barely. There was a pink flush to her cheeks. She looked very warm and cozy.

"What time is it?" she mumbled.

"It's five. I have to go to the hospital." He kissed her bare shoulder, groaning inwardly again, not wanting to leave.

She sat up quickly. "What's wrong?"

"A trauma is coming in and they need all hands on deck." Gavin cupped her face and kissed her again. "I'm sure if they need the chief of surgery, they'll page you. For now, why don't you just lie back and rest?"

Virginia snorted. "As if. If there's a trauma coming in, I'll be there."

Gavin watched as she scrambled out of bed, the sheet wrapped around her. "You know, you don't have to be so coy with me in the morning. Not after last night."

Virginia's cheeks flushed pink. "It was dark last night."

"You're a prude." He winked.

"Not at all." Then, as if to prove her point, she dropped the sheet, showing off every inch of her naked body to him.

Gavin's sex stirred and he groaned. "You're killing me."

"You're the one who called me a prude." She slipped on her lace panties and then pulled on her dress. "Are you going to just lie there with a trauma coming in?"

"Turn around."

"Now who's the prude?" she asked, teasing him.

"Fine." He stood up and her eyes widened at the sight of him, naked and aroused. Her blush deepened and she turned away.

"A little warning would've been nice."

"I warned you." He waggled his eyebrows when she glanced back at him.

"Get dressed and I'll meet you downstairs." She grinned at him as she collected her purse and left the room.

Gavin quickly pulled on the necessary components of his tux and carried the rest. Virginia was downstairs and was just finishing with the check-out.

A cab was hailed by the doorman and they slid in the back together. The atmosphere became tense and Gavin couldn't figure out why, but Virginia was barely glancing at him and she was sitting ramrod straight almost right against the opposite door.

"Are you okay?"

"Fine," she said, but there was a nervous edge to her voice.

"What changed between the hotel room and here?"

"The taxi driver." Virginia winked and then she lowered her voice. "Last night was wonderful, Gavin, but right now there's a huge trauma coming in and we need all our wits about us."

"I think coffee is in order. I didn't get much sleep last night."

The cab driver smirked in the front seat and Virginia shot him a warning look.

"This is me being a prude again. Seriously, we can't have people gossiping."

He was tempted to say, "Who the heck cares?", but he didn't. He knew Virginia as the chief of surgery had a professional image to keep up.

"Okay, you have my word. I'll be good…for now." And then he snatched her hand and kissed it.

Virginia smiled and touched his face. "Your scruffies are back."

Gavin laughed. "Well, I didn't have time to shave."

When the cab driver pulled up to the emergency room doors at Bayview Grace there were already four ambulances pulled up out front.

"Go," Virginia said. "I'll take care of this. I have to swing around to the front to change. You'd better change into scrubs too. That's a rental."

Gavin nodded and jumped out of the cab. He ran into the emergency room and headed straight for the locker rooms. He peeled off his tux, jammed it into his locker and pulled out a fresh set of scrubs and his running shoes.

Once he was suitably dressed he headed back out into the fray.

"What do we got, people?" he shouted over the din.

"Multi-vehicle accident on the freeway." Kimber, the charge nurse on duty, handed him a clipboard. "The less critical cases are being sent here as the nearest hospital is full up."

Gavin nodded. A gurney was coming in and he ran to catch up to the paramedics. "Status?"

"Jennifer Coi, age thirty, was a restrained driver in a multi-car pileup. Vitals are good, but she's complaining of tenderness over the abdomen and pain in her neck."

"Take her to pod one," Gavin ordered.

He glanced around the emergency room, which was humming with activity. This was nothing as traumatic as the other hospital was probably getting, but he couldn't see how the board could or would close this department down.

Bayview Grace's ER was needed in this end of the city. Only truly heartless, greedy people would shut it down. He shuddered because that was the impression he got from Edwin Schultz. Greedy. If that man had been a cartoon character, he'd have permanent dollar signs in his eyes.

Dollar signs Gavin wanted to smack off his face.

Lives mattered more than the almighty dollar. That was what he'd learned in the field. Only more dollars would've brought better medicine to a lot of those developing countries.

It was a vicious cycle.

*Focus.*

Gavin shook those thoughts from his head. There was no time to think about budgets and politics. Right now, Mrs. Coi was his priority.

Life over limb.

Mrs. Coi needed him to be alert and in the game.

This was why he'd become a doctor, to save lives.

This was all that mattered to him.

Before he ducked into pod one to deal with his patient he caught sight of Virginia coming from the direction of her office, in scrubs and with her hair hastily tied back, examining individuals on the beds in the main room. They hadn't paged her and she could've just stayed in bed, but she'd jumped into the fray without complaint.

It was just one more thing he loved about her.


Mrs. Coi's condition was a lot worse than original triage at the accident site had indicated. Her spleen had been on the verge of rupturing, so Gavin and Dr. Jefferson had wheeled her into emergency surgery.

Gavin had got to the woman just in the nick of time. He'd removed her spleen and was now closing up.

"How was the benefit last night?" Jefferson asked as they worked over Mrs. Coi. The question shocked him. He was not one for idle chitchat in the operating room.

"It went really well." He cleared his throat. "Why?"

"I heard your speech was something to hear, that's all," Jefferson said offhandedly.

"Clamp." He held out his hand and the scrub nurse handed it to him. "I don't know about that."

Jefferson's eyebrows rose. "I've heard nothing but great

things about your speech, Gavin. I only wish *I* could've been there to hear it personally."

Gavin just shot him a look of disbelief as he really couldn't frown his disapproval behind a surgical mask. He wasn't going to get into this with him.

"More suction, please, Dr. Jefferson."

Jefferson suctioned around the artery and Gavin began to close the layers.

"I did hear something very interesting last night, though." The way he'd said "something very interesting" made Gavin's hackles rise.

What had he heard? Had anyone seen him and Virginia going to the elevator or had someone seen them this morning, leaving in a cab together?

"Did you?" He was hoping his tone conveyed that he wasn't in the least bit interested in pursuing this topic of conversation.

"Yes, according to Janice, the ice queen is leaving Bayview Grace."

"What?" Gavin paused in mid-suturing. "Sorry. Dr. Potter is leaving Bayview Grace?"

Jefferson's eyes narrowed. "Dr. Brice, are you going to continue to close?"

He shook his head. "Yes, but continue what you heard. I'm all ears."

"Ice Queen was offered a job at some fancy Boston hospital. They're offering her a huge salary and lots of research grants. It's also a level-one trauma center."

Gavin's stomach dropped to the soles of his feet and his head began to swim. How many times had Virginia reiterated that her career was important to her? Her job was everything, and if a Boston hospital was offering her a heck of a lot more, why would she stay?

*Maybe that's why she seduced me.*

That thought angered him, but it made sense. She'd constantly rebuffed him, telling him they couldn't be in a relationship because she was essentially his boss, but last night she'd been the one to drag him upstairs to the room.

The one who'd kissed him. She'd been the one who'd wanted him last night. Oh, he'd wanted it too, but he hadn't been going to press her. He hadn't wanted to scare her off, especially after how she'd made it so clear that they couldn't be together in that way.

"Did she accept the job?"

"I don't know, but I heard Janice talking about it to another nurse last night. Janice was gushing to anyone who would listen about how proud she was of Dr. Potter and how she was going to miss her." Jefferson snorted. "Well, I'm not going to miss the ice queen. Good riddance, as far as I'm concerned."

Gavin gritted his teeth and took a deep calming breath, because he was suturing up the subcutaneous layer and because he didn't want Jefferson or any of the other staff to know this news affected him.

Only it did.

After what they'd shared last night, Gavin was positive something was going to come of it, but if she was going to move to Boston...

*You don't know that. It's all hearsay.*

"Would you finish closing for me, Dr. Jefferson?"

"Of course, Dr. Brice."

Jefferson took over the suturing and Gavin left the operating room. He tossed his gloves in the medical waste and jammed his scrub gown in the laundry basket. After he'd finished scrubbing out he headed straight for Virginia's office, hoping she'd be there.

What Jefferson was saying could be just idle prattle. The only one who could confirm it was Virginia. He hoped it was just a rumor.

He hoped she hadn't just slept with him because he was one last fling and that it was okay to have sex with him because she was going to leave Bayview Grace and San Francisco.

There was no way he could go to Boston. He wasn't going

to uproot his nieces on the off chance Virginia wanted more from him.

And he wasn't going to go through another custody battle with their grandparents. The only reason he'd won the last one had been because he planned to remain in San Francisco and give them the stability Casey had so desperately wanted for them.

Gavin wasn't going to risk all of that for idle gossip, or for someone who'd just used him. Who didn't really want him.

Janice wasn't at her desk, but he could see that Virginia was in her office, bent over her desk and working on files.

He didn't knock, he just barged in. She looked up at him, momentarily surprised, but then grinned. "Gavin, I heard you were in surgery for a ruptured spleen. How did it go?"

"It went fine," he snapped.

"Is something wrong?" Virginia frowned and set down her file.

"Are you taking that job in Boston or what?"

Virginia's mouth dropped open. "What're you talking about?"

Gavin shut her office door. "I heard you were offered a nice job in Boston. One with lots of nice research funding."

She frowned. "Where did you hear that?"

"Dr. Jefferson."

"And how did Dr. Jefferson find out?"

Gavin's stomach twisted. "So it's true. You've been offered a position."

"I'm not going to deny it, so yes. Yes, I have, and it's a very nice offer."

Gavin crossed his arms. "I see."

"A friend recommended me for an opening."

"So it's a good offer?"

"Yes," Virginia said. "It's tempting."

"Did you accept?"

Her mouth opened and she was about to answer but her office phone rang. "Dr. Potter speaking. Yes, Mr. Schultz. Of course, I'll be up momentarily."

"The board?"

"Yes, they want to meet with me." Virginia didn't look at him as she picked up her white lab coat and slipped it over her scrubs. "I have to go, Gavin. Can we talk about this later?"

"I think I have all the information I need."

Gavin left her office. She hadn't denied or confirmed anything, meaning that she probably was going to take the job and move across the country. He was angry at himself for letting her in when he'd known he shouldn't. Virginia was career driven, but mostly he was angry that he'd allowed the girls to get to know her.

And that rested solely with him. It was his fault and the guilt of allowing that to happen was eating him up inside.

"First off, Dr. Potter, we'd like to thank you for organizing such a great benefit last night. Even though it was a huge success, the investors still feel like their money would be better put to use if we turned Bayview Grace into a private clinic." Mr. Schultz gave her a pat on the back and then returned to his seat at the end of the long table. "We're cutting the trauma department. We've decided to turn the emergency room into a plastic day-surgery suite."

"Plastic day surgery?" she said.

"Botox and skin-tag removal. Clinics like that prove to be the most lucrative." Mr. Schultz grinned and started going on and on about his plans for turning her emergency room into a spa.

*Botox and skin tags?* Virginia had to repeat the words in her mind again because she couldn't get a grip on the reality of it.

Was that what her emergency room was being reduced to? Two years of hard work, late nights and sacrifice to salvage a wreck of a hospital, to bring it up to national standards, and it was all being wiped clean. Excised like a blemish on the face of San Francisco.

Virginia's heart sank, but she was also angry. She didn't know why she bothered wasting her time and wasting the time of all those surgeons who had given such excellent speeches. It had been an exercise in futility. Just like she'd feared it would be. "I see, and what other departments will be cut?"

"Just the emergency department. It's the one that bleeds the most money. We have people just wandering in off the streets and there's no guarantee that billing could track them down and get them to pay."

"And what of the staff in the trauma department?"

Mr. Schultz tented his fingers, the sunlight filtering through the slatted blinds reflecting against his shiny bald head, making him look like one of those evil villains from an old cartoon or an old James Bond movie. "They'll be given a generous severance package as per their contracts. We really don't have the spots for them. We're planning to recruit some of the top plastic surgeons in the country. We are aware you're primarily a trauma surgeon but we'd like you to stay on as Chief of Surgery."

Virginia closed her eyes and all she could see was Shyanne's face in her casket. She couldn't afford the health care she'd needed and it had cost her her life. Then she thought of Gavin and the girls. What would become of them?

She couldn't work for a hospital like this, for a board of directors who only wanted to help people who had the money to pay. Growing up in a poor family—well, she'd been a victim of such exclusivity before and she wasn't going to work for an employer who believed in it.

It went against everything her father had taught her, but she knew for the first time she was going to have to quit without the promise of another job, because she wasn't going to take that job in Boston either.

She wanted to stay in San Francisco with Gavin. Maybe she'd open up her own urgent-care clinic somewhere down in the Mission district, where she could give help to those who needed it. It frightened her, but also gave her a thrill.

"I'm sorry, Mr. Schultz, but I'm going to have to decline."

"Pardon?" he said. "What do you mean, decline?"

"I mean I'm quitting. I'll give you my six weeks' notice, but after that I'm done. I can't work for a private hospital."

Mr. Schultz shrugged. "Very well, but before you go you have to tell the trauma department what the board's decision is. We want the ER closed by the end of this week."

Virginia's stomach twisted. She'd never had to fire so many people in her life, but she had little choice. The axe was dropping on Bayview Grace and there was nothing she could do about it. "Fine, I'll tell them tomorrow. They're still dealing with a large trauma that has come in."

Mr. Schultz wrinkled his nose. "Yes, I'm aware of that."

Virginia nodded and left the boardroom. Mr. Schultz didn't thank her for her years of service, or anything else for that matter, and she didn't care. She never had liked the head of the board.

Janice was at her desk when Virginia returned and she looked anxious.

"Well, what's the word, Dr. Potter?" she asked in a hushed undertone.

Virginia just shook her head.

Janice's face paled. "No."

"I'm afraid so."

"When?" Janice asked, her voice barely more than a whisper.

"By the end of this week. I have to tell the staff tomorrow."

"That's—that's crappy."

"Your words, my sentiments."

"I'm sorry, Dr. Potter. Truly I am. I wouldn't wish that job on my worst enemy."

"Thanks, Janice." Virginia scrubbed her hand over her face, feeling emotionally drained and exhausted. She let out a long sigh. "If anyone wants me, I'll be in my office. I need some time to think."

"Speaking of enemies, Dr. Brice is in there. He's been waiting since you went up to your meeting. He looks quite agitated."

Virginia groaned inwardly. "Thanks, Janice." She opened the door and Gavin spun around to face her. He'd been looking out her window, the one that overlooked the garden courtyard.

"What did the board say?"

"If I tell you, you can't say anything to your staff until I make my announcement to them tomorrow. I mean it, Gavin."

His brow furrowed. "You can't be serious. After everything that happened last night, they're going to axe the trauma department?"

Virginia scrubbed her hand over her face. "Yes."

Gavin cursed under his breath. "You're going to tell the rest of the staff tomorrow?"

"Yes, everyone is being let go in that department. The board wants to start fresh and they want the budget to hire top-of-the-line plastic surgeons to come to Bayview Grace."

Gavin snorted. "Plastic surgeons?"

"They're going to turn the ER into a plastic day-clinic/spa thing."

"Just what the city needs, more botox clinics. Of all the stupid, moronic… It's just plain dumb. What a bunch of heartless money-mongers."

Virginia sat down in her chair, suddenly completely exhausted. "Your words, my thoughts exactly. I'm sorry this had to happen to you, Gavin. Hopefully, you won't lose custody of the girls."

"What?" he snapped, his eyes narrowed and flashing with anger. "What did you say?"

Virginia cursed inwardly, knowing she'd overstepped her bounds by reading that document, but there was no going back now.

"The custody battle with the girls' grandparents. I saw the

judgment stipulated that you had to remain in employment here in San Francisco or you could lose custody of the girls."

"How do you know that?" Gavin demanded, his voice rising in anger.

"I read the judgment."

"How dared you read that? That was private."

Virginia stood up. "It fell off the fridge and I picked it up. If you wanted to keep it private you shouldn't have left it in your kitchen, where anyone could see it."

"It doesn't matter where it was, that was none of your business."

Virginia pinched the bridge of her nose. "Why are you making such a big deal about it?"

"Because it was private. You're not part of my family or the girls'. You had no right to go prying."

"I'm sorry."

Gavin snorted. "Sorry doesn't cut it."

"I thought we meant something more to each other."

"Yeah, well, that was before your job offer in Boston and you prying into things you had no business to." Gavin strode across the room and opened the door. "I won't say a word to the staff, but I hope you enjoy the east coast, Dr. Potter."

"I'm not taking the job, Gavin. I want to stay in San Francisco."

"You should take that job in Boston. There's nothing left here for you." And with those parting words he slammed the door to her office and to her heart.

Virginia didn't sleep well. When she dragged herself into the hospital she saw that the notice was already taped to the ER's doors. Last night when they'd had a slow period she'd called Ambulance Dispatch and told them that Bayview Grace was closing its emergency room. Then she'd asked Security to lock all the doors and tape the notices up.

The nurses and doctors on duty had been dumbfounded.

When all the patients had left, she'd told them she'd speak to them in the morning when the morning shift came in.

She hadn't even gone home that night. Instead she spent the night on the couch in her office, but sleep hadn't come to her. Her mind had just kept racing. Two thoughts plagued her. The layoff speech and Gavin's dismissal of her.

*"You should take that job in Boston. There is nothing for you here."*

It had stunned her and broken her heart.

*Why did I read that judgment?*

She kept chastising herself over and over again. In the early hours of the morning she'd finally realized she had been in the wrong for reading the custody judgment, but Gavin had totally overreacted. He'd won the judgment. There was nothing to be ashamed about.

Closing her out and ending what they'd had was immature. Especially without giving her the benefit of an explanation.

She deserved to have her explanation heard after all they'd had.

*What had they had?*

That was the crux. There had been no firm commitment in their relationship. All they'd had was one night of wanton abandon and the odd pleasant discourse.

No. Not just the odd conversation. Virginia had thought at the very least they were friends. She didn't have many girlfriends, but from what she understood, friends gave friends the benefit of the doubt.

Virginia shook her head in the bathroom mirror and then finished brushing her teeth. She'd thought Gavin had at least been her friend, but apparently she'd been wrong.

It was just better for her when she had no connections. When it was just her and the pathetic cactus in her apartment.

Relationships were messy and needy. Virginia didn't have time for all this stuff.

Only she'd never felt more alive or happy as she had these

past few weeks that she'd been with Gavin, and now it was all gone.

Janice knocked on the door and opened it. "Dr. Potter?"

Virginia rinsed her toothbrush and walked out of her office bathroom. "Yes, Janice."

"The trauma department staff are waiting for you in board-room three." Janice gave her a weak smile and turned to leave, but then stopped and walked toward her.

"Is there something you need, Janice?" Virginia asked, confused by Janice's demure manner.

"I just wanted to tell you that I'm going to miss you, Dr. Potter. I've enjoyed working with you."

Virginia was confused. She hadn't told Janice about her decision to leave. She had been planning to tell her after she dealt with closing down the ER. She didn't want the trauma staff to think she was playing the martyr for them.

"Where did you hear that I was leaving?"

"Mr. Schultz asked me to post an advertisement for your position amongst the other senior attendings who are staying."

Virginia pinched the bridge of her nose. "I was going to tell you."

Janice nodded. "I know, and I understand why you were keeping it a secret, but now the staff know."

Virginia sighed and then two arms wrapped around her. It was Janice hugging her. Just that simple act of human contact caused Virginia to break down in tears. She'd never mourned her sister properly. She'd never had time, but even that was coming out of her.

It was like a dam had exploded and everything she was feeling, that she'd pent up inside for too long, came gushing out of her, washing her clean.

Janice just held her, patting her back and whispering soothing words to her. How everything was going to be okay and that she understood Virginia had to do it.

When the sobbing finally ceased, Janice let go of her firm grip on Virginia and smoothed back her hair.

"I know it's not my place, you being my boss and all, but I do think of you as a daughter, Virginia."

It was the first time Janice had really used her name. Virginia returned the wobbly smile. "Thanks, Janice."

"No, I mean it. I remember when you came in for your interview as a resident. You were so aloof and like a robot. That's where you earned the nickname Ice Queen. You displayed no emotions, no empathy, but these last couple of months..." Janice shook her head and smiled. "You're not an ice queen any more. You don't deserve that name. The Dr. Virginia Potter who first started here wouldn't be as compassionate about what she has to do now. I like you so much better this way and I'm really going to miss this woman."

"Janice, I don't think I can do this. I fought so hard to bring that department up to level-one standards and now I'm pulling the plug on it. The board signed a DNR and I'm unhooking it from life support."

Janice's brow furrowed. "That's the corniest thing you've ever said to me."

Virginia laughed and brushed away a few errant tears with the back of her hand. "Sorry, my brain is a little fried."

"I noticed, but something else is going on."

"I slept with Gavin."

Janice's eyes widened and then she nodded. "I thought so. The way he looks at you and the way you look at him. Look, I don't think he'll be angry at you, he'll understand why you have to lay him off. He's a bit of an ass and clueless when it comes to social interactions with the staff, but I don't think he's cold-hearted."

Tears stung Virginia's eyes again. "It's over; it was over before it really got started."

"I don't understand."

"Gavin overreacted to something I did and basically rejected me."

Janice cocked an eyebrow. "What did you do?"

"I can't say what it was. It was nothing bad. I just read something private that I shouldn't have. It fell off the fridge at his place and I picked it up and read it. He was livid."

Janice snorted. "Then he shouldn't have left it on the fridge. What is wrong with men? The next time I see him I'm going to give him a piece of my mind."

"No, don't do that," Virginia said. "Then he'll get angrier that I told someone about it. Just let it be. It was never meant to work out anyway. I can see that now."

"Okay," Janice said. "You know, you really look wiped."

"I didn't get much sleep last night and I feel like I've aged about ten years."

"You've got some deep shadows around your eyes. I'd put on some concealer if I were you." Janice winked. "It won't be smooth sailing today, I'm not going to lie to you, but don't let them bully you."

Virginia gave Janice a peck on the cheek. "Thanks."

"You're welcome." Janice opened the door and turned. "If you set up another practice somewhere I can be bought for the right amount of money and vacation time." Janice winked and left.

Virginia scrubbed her hand over her face and headed back to the bathroom. Her face was blotchy and red. Her eyes were bloodshot. She looked and felt like she was a hundred years old. She couldn't help but wonder how many gray hairs from this ordeal she was going to get.

At least it would soon be over. The ER doctors and staff would get their severance packages and they'd be gone.

All she would have to do was paperwork and tie up some loose ends. Then she could walk away from Bayview Grace.

And go where? She didn't know.

She had no interest in going to Boston.

She felt like she was in limbo and it terrified her.

Virginia splashed some water on her face and pulled her hair back into a ponytail. She held her head high when she left her office, Janice giving her an encouraging smile, which she appreciated immensely.

*Shoulders back and head held high, Virginia.*

Her hand paused on the knob of the boardroom door. She could hear the rumbling murmurs from those who were about to lose their jobs, through the door.

*You can do this.*

Steeling her resolve, she pushed open the door and stepped into the room. The large boardroom was full. All the seats were taken and there were several people standing along the walls. In the crowd she picked out Gavin right away. He was looking at her, but there was no warmth to his gaze.

It was like she was looking at a stranger. A cold, distant stranger, and that made her heart clench.

The room fell silent and every eye in that room was on her. She could feel them boring into her back. She walked up to the front of the room.

"I'm glad you could all make it. I want to discuss the reasons I closed down the emergency room last night. The board of Bayview Grace Hospital has decided to turn Bayview into a private hospital. One that doesn't have a trauma department."

"What?" someone shouted, and an explosion of angry voices began to talk amongst themselves and at her.

Virginia held up her hand. "I know. I understand your frustrations."

"But what about that benefit?" Kimber asked. "I don't understand. I heard that it went well."

Virginia nodded. "It did, Kimber, but the investors who signed on agree with the board's decision to turn this into a profitable private hospital."

"So what's going to happen to the ER?" Dr. Jefferson asked. "Is it just going to be wasted space?"

"It will be turned into a plastic surgery-day spa."

"What does that mean?" someone shouted angrily from the back.

"It doesn't matter what it means. It's done. The board is hiring plastic surgeons this minute and Dr. Watkinson from Plastics is being made head of that department."

"What's going to happen to us?" Kimber asked, her voice tiny in the din.

Virginia glanced at Gavin. His eyes looked hooded and dark from across the room, but then she saw a momentary glimmer of sympathy.

She looked at Kimber. "I'm afraid, effective immediately, you've all been made redundant here at Bayview Grace."

Kimber's face fell and she looked like she was on the verge of tears. Tears Virginia herself was trying to hold back. The angry voices increased, but she kept her focus on Kimber.

Or, as Gavin had referred to her, Hello Kitty. She was wearing those scrubs now. Virginia had always liked Kimber. She was one of the many staff Virginia liked and was sad to see go.

"Tomorrow you may all pick up your severance packages. You will each find a letter of recommendation from me."

"You tried, Dr. Potter," Kimber said.

Virginia paused as she tried to leave the room and met Kimber's gaze.

"We know how hard you worked to save our jobs."

Virginia glanced at the faces of her staff and, except for the odd irate doctor, all she saw was sympathy and compassion. Even gratitude for what she'd tried to do. It made tears well up in her eyes, but when she looked for affirmation from Gavin, the one person she cared about, she found none.

Gavin had left the room.

*What did you expect?*

Virginia then knew it was definitely over. He was done and so was she.

# CHAPTER EIGHTEEN

*Six weeks later*

"YOU NEED TO get out of this funk, Dr. Brice," Rosalie chastised him. "You're seriously starting to depress me. I don't understand what you're so upset about. Your urgent care clinic is running smoothly and you have more hours now to spend with the girls."

Gavin sighed and poured himself another cup of coffee. She was right. He'd been in a funk since his *stupid* fight with Virginia.

He'd thought about calling her but hadn't. He'd been such an idiot.

"You're right, Rosalie. I'm sorry for bumming you out."

Rosalie *tsked* under her breath. "It's Dr. Potter, isn't it? Have you talked to her?"

"No. I haven't spoken to her since I was handed my severance package." Even then it hadn't been Virginia who'd handed him the severance package, it had been Janice, who'd given him the stink-eye when she did it.

"I still don't understand what happened." Rosalie shook her head. "I could've sworn that woman cared for you. I'm usually never wrong about these things."

"I overreacted. I was tired, emotionally drained and I overreacted. I blew my chance because of my temper." And then he proceeded to tell Rosalie the entire story of what had happened between him and Virginia the last time they'd spoken.

Rosalie let out a string of Spanish curses, all of which he was sure were aimed at him and were probably different words for idiot.

When her tirade subsided she crossed her arms over her ample bosom and glared at him. Her dark eyes were flinty. "You need to go and see her before she leaves San Francisco and you never see her again."

"She won't want to see me."

"Ah, you're so stubborn. It drives me crazy." Rosalie began to curse again and then marched over to him and pinched his cheek, shaking him hard. "You need to apologize to her. So what she read the judgment? She was right. You left it in a stupid place and, frankly, I think it meant she cared."

"She was offered a job in Boston and slept with me on the same night. Don't you find that suspicious?"

"No, I don't. I saw the way she looked at you and the way you looked at her. The job offer and you two finally getting together were just coincidences. I know she cared for you. It's just you're a man, you're *stupido.*"

"*Stupido* I will take. You could've called me worse."

A smile cracked on Rosalie's lips. "Believe me, I want to."

Gavin groaned. "I miss her."

"So do I."

Rosalie let out a shriek and Gavin spun around, spilling coffee down the front of his shirt. Rose had climbed out of bed and was standing in the doorway of the kitchen. In her hand was Georgiana.

"Rose, what did you say?" Gavin asked as he knelt down in front of her.

"I miss Virginia." Then she gave Georgiana a little squeak right in his face. Gavin pulled his niece tight against him, hugging her. She'd spoken. The last time he'd heard her voice had been just before Casey's death.

*"I want my mommy."*

*"I know you do, Rose."*

It was the last thing she'd said. It had haunted him daily since she'd gone silent. He'd been worried she'd forget how to talk or, worse, that they'd forget what her voice sounded like.

The doctors called it selective mutism, but no matter what Gavin had done, he hadn't been able to coax Rose to talk.

Right now, her voice had a lilt of a thousand angels.

"I'm hungry and you're squishing me." She squirmed out of Gavin's arms and climbed up to the table.

"What do you want for breakfast, *querida*?" Rosalie asked through some choked sobs.

"Cereal."

"Then that's what you shall have." Rosalie covered her face with her hands and sobbed silently, her back to them, her shoulders shaking.

"What's wrong, Rosalie?" Rose asked. "Why are you sad?"

Rosalie laughed. Her voice was wobbly. "I'm not sad, *querida.* You make me so happy. Now, what kind of cereal?"

"Chocolate!" Rose's eyes twinkled as Rosalie grabbed a bowl and poured Rose a bowl of chocolate puffs.

Gavin brushed away a few of his own tears as he stood up.

Rose had made perfect sense and had stated the obvious. And Lily had been in a foul mood for a long time, as had he.

Virginia had brought a light to their lives. One he couldn't deny any more.

He'd never thought he'd find someone he wanted to settle down with, but then again he'd never thought he'd be raising children. When he'd pictured his life, he'd imagined that he'd be working until he died in some far-flung country.

Now that life was not one he wanted.

He wanted the stability that Casey had achieved. He wanted family and someone he loved to come home to.

He wanted Virginia.

"I'm going out."

Rosalie grinned. "Are you going where I think you're going?"

Gavin nodded. "Yeah, I'm going to go make things right."

Virginia worked her last shift at Bayview Grace in the evening, only because she didn't want to face Janice and all the others during the day. She didn't want them to see her cry. She tied up the loose ends she needed to in the peace and quiet of the night shift. There was no one in the trauma department. All of the staff were long gone.

Word about her leaving Bayview Grace was actually met, for the most part, with sorrow. No one wanted to see her go.

The board had hired Dr. Watkinson as their chief of surgery and he was already out ordering people around and making changes, all with Edwin Schultz's glowing affirmation.

Even though, technically, Virginia was still Chief of Surgery, she just let Dr. Watkinson have his way, because she'd emotionally disconnected herself from the hospital the moment she'd laid off all those employees.

Dr. Watkinson had hired some of them back, nurses he was fond of, but not everyone. Kimber, for instance, was gone. There was no smiling face down in the ER any more. No more "Hello Kitty" scrubs directing paramedics where to go.

Of course there was no ER.

And as she walked through it on her last day the scene with Mr. Jones and the board replayed in her mind and now she could laugh about it.

She could see it all so clearly. Gavin cracking that man's chest with such skill and precision. Not caring that the board and a handful of investors were watching with horror on their faces.

*"Life over limb."*

It was his motto and it was a good motto. Mr. Jones had survived.

Maybe if Shyanne had got herself to a hospital when she'd first started having shoulder pain she would've come across a trauma surgeon like Gavin and her life might have been spared by a simple operation. They just would've removed the fallopian tube.

Virginia sighed and left the ER. Heading back to her office, or rather Dr. Watkinson's office. When she got up there she could see him in her old office, measuring something.

She just shook her head.

Janice stood. "I couldn't keep him out of there a moment longer. I took your box and purse out. I figured you wouldn't want to go in there and talk to him."

"I appreciate that, Janice. I've talked to him enough this week about the job." Virginia rolled her eyes.

"What're you going to do now? I know you turned down that job in Boston."

Virginia shrugged. "I don't know. Maybe I'll open a private practice somewhere, but first things first. I'm going to go home and visit with my family."

"South Dakota?"

"Yep." Though it was not really home to her anymore. San Francisco, Gavin and the girls felt like a real home to her, but that was all gone. She hadn't seen him in weeks. Not since the layoffs and their gazes had locked across the room. She'd thought she'd seen a glimmer of sympathy there, but she must've been wrong.

"How long have you been away?" Janice asked.

"I haven't been back there..." She hesitated like she always did when she came close to mentioning Shyanne. "I haven't been home since my sister died. It was too painful, but now I feel resolved. I feel like a huge weight has been lifted from my shoulders."

Janice hugged her. "I'm really going to miss you, Dr. Potter."

"I'm going to miss you too, Janice."

Janice nodded and smiled. "Don't worry. I won't make things easy on Dr. Watkinson." With the mischievous glint in Janice's eyes, Virginia was prone to believe her.

"Well, I'd better be going. I'm officially no longer an employee here." She handed over her hospital ID and key card. "I'd better leave and make this less painful. The exit interview was bad enough. Goodbye, Janice."

Virginia picked up her box of belongings. Throughout the week she'd taken larger items home. All that remained were the few things she'd needed to get her through until the end.

And now it was here.

As she walked through the halls of the hospital that had been her passion, the very center of her being for so long, she didn't feel sad.

When she stepped outside an unseasonably warm breeze caressed her face and she sighed.

She turned back, only once, and looked up at Bayview Grace, staring the hospital she'd tried to save. A few months ago she would've been sad to walk away, but now she just felt resolved to Bayview's fate. In retrospect there was nothing she could've done.

She'd done everything right.

She'd done her best.

She felt nervous that she didn't have a job yet, but she was sure she could find something in San Francisco. In the interim she'd booked a trip to return to De Smet and visit her family.

It was something that was long overdue; she had to put the ghost of her sister to rest.

And she wouldn't mind having the company of her large family in a confined space for a bit. It would be better than staring at the walls in her apartment. She hadn't realized how much she'd miss Gavin until he was gone.

She wasn't angry at him any more, she just missed him.

They were both too stubborn and settled in their ways to be together—at least, that's what she told herself.

Kids and a husband hadn't ever been in her original plans, but life could change in an instant. Something she'd learned from working in trauma her whole career, but she hadn't really understood it until Gavin Brice and his two nieces had come barging into her life.

The box under her arm was heavy and she shifted it, pulling out her car keys. With a sigh of resignation she turned around to head to her car and froze in her tracks.

Gavin was in the parking lot, leaning against his motorcycle and dressed in his leathers. He was parked right next to her sedan.

Her knees knocked with nervousness, while the rest of her body was excited to see him. She wanted to throw herself into his arms, but after his parting words to her she refrained from making such a fool of herself.

Instead she walked over to him, opened her car and shoved her box of belongings inside. "Hello, Dr. Brice."

"Dr. Potter," he acknowledged. "Coming off the night shift?"

"Yes."

"I'm glad it was the night shift. I didn't really relish waiting here all day."

"What are you doing here?"

Gavin took off his sunglasses. "I've come to apologize."

Her eyes widened in shock. She leaned against her car. "I'm listening."

"I'm sorry, I was just angry about losing my job and…well, I wasn't angry that you read that judgment. I was angrier about the fact that I could lose you."

"To the Boston job?"

"Yes, but by the time you told me you weren't taking it my temper had gotten away with me. I was an idiot."

A smile quirked her lips. "I agree with that."

Gavin chuckled. "I've been trying to apologize for a couple of weeks now. I just… As I said, I was an idiot."

"Yes, so you said. I'm sorry too, Gavin. I shouldn't have pried, but I care for you and the girls. So much."

"They care for you too. Rose said she missed you."

"What?" Virginia was stunned. "Rose spoke?"

Gavin nodded. "This morning. She said she misses you, and Lily has been in a foul mood for weeks."

A lump formed in Virginia's throat. "I miss them too. I never thought kids liked me too much and vice versa, but I do miss your girls."

Gavin took a step forward, taking her hands in his. "Is that all, just the girls?"

Her heart began to race. "I've missed you too, Gavin. So much."

He cupped her cheeks and kissed her. Virginia's knees went weak and she melted into him, her whole body feeling like gelatin, almost like the earth below her feet was shaking, but it wasn't an earthquake she was feeling. She was feeling relief, love and joy.

Gavin broke off the kiss and leaned his forehead against hers. "I've missed you, Virginia. I fought my feelings so many times. I didn't want to settle down, but I can't help it. I love you."

"I love you too, Gavin…against my better judgment," she teased.

He laughed and kissed her again, holding her tight against his body. "Why don't we head back to my place? We can come back for your car later. That is, unless you have any other plans?"

"No, nothing. Even though it terrifies me to the very core, I'm unemployed."

"I have an opening at my clinic."

Virginia cocked an eyebrow. "Your clinic?"

He nodded. "I took my severance money, got some investors and opened an urgent-care clinic not far from here. I hired as many staff members from Bayview's trauma as I could. Kimber is head nurse now!"

Virginia was pleased. "That's—that's wonderful. Kimber is an excellent nurse. What else do you have at your clinic?"

"We have an OR and can do most minor surgeries. I also have a generous enough budget to do pro bono work. So, what do you say? Would you like a job?"

This time Virginia kissed him. She couldn't remember the

last time she'd felt so happy, so free. The job he was offering wouldn't pay as much as Bayview or the Boston hospital would, but she'd be doing a job that would help out people like Shyanne and that was worth its weight in gold.

"When do I start?"

"I'm headed there right now." Gavin handed her a helmet. "But you're just coming off the night shift."

Virginia took the helmet and jammed it on her head. "I'm a surgeon. I'm ready. Although I will have to cancel my trip to De Smet next week."

"You were going to visit your family?"

"Yeah, but I can cancel it."

"No, you're going, and Lily and Rose could use a bit of a holiday. Don't they have a Laura Ingalls Wilder museum there?"

"They do."

"Then I think we should all take a trip out there."

"Are you sure? It'll be cold this time of year."

"Positive. I want to meet your family, because all I want is you, Virginia. Just you."

She wrapped her arms around his neck and kissed his scruffy face. "Did I tell you how much I love you and your scruffies?"

"Yes, but tell me again."

Virginia grinned and kissed him again. "So much."

Gavin nodded. "Ditto. Let's go check out your new job, Dr. Potter."

Virginia climbed onto the back of his motorcycle, wrapping her arms around his chest. "I'm ready, Dr. Brice."

And with him, she was. She was ready for anything.

\* \* \* \* \*

## *Mills & Boon® Hardback*
### *February 2014*

# ROMANCE

| | |
|---|---|
| A Bargain with the Enemy | Carole Mortimer |
| A Secret Until Now | Kim Lawrence |
| Shamed in the Sands | Sharon Kendrick |
| Seduction Never Lies | Sara Craven |
| When Falcone's World Stops Turning | Abby Green |
| Securing the Greek's Legacy | Julia James |
| An Exquisite Challenge | Jennifer Hayward |
| A Debt Paid in Passion | Dani Collins |
| The Last Guy She Should Call | Joss Wood |
| No Time Like Mardi Gras | Kimberly Lang |
| Daring to Trust the Boss | Susan Meier |
| Rescued by the Millionaire | Cara Colter |
| Heiress on the Run | Sophie Pembroke |
| The Summer They Never Forgot | Kandy Shepherd |
| Trouble On Her Doorstep | Nina Harrington |
| Romance For Cynics | Nicola Marsh |
| Melting the Ice Queen's Heart | Amy Ruttan |
| Resisting Her Ex's Touch | Amber McKenzie |

# MEDICAL

| | |
|---|---|
| Tempted by Dr Morales | Carol Marinelli |
| The Accidental Romeo | Carol Marinelli |
| The Honourable Army Doc | Emily Forbes |
| A Doctor to Remember | Joanna Neil |